THE SKELETON RIDERS

THE SKELETON RIDERS

JACKSON COLE

WHEELER
CHIVERS

This Large Print edition is published by Wheeler Publishing, Waterville, Maine, USA and by BBC Audiobooks Ltd, Bath, England.
Wheeler Publishing, a part of Gale, Cengage Learning.
Copyright © 1950 by Leslie Scott.
Copyright © renewed 1978 by Lily Scott.
The moral right of the author has been asserted.

LIBRARY OF CONGRESS CATALOGING-IN-PUBLICATION DATA

Cole, Jackson.
   The skeleton riders / by Jackson Cole.
     p. cm. — (Wheeler Publishing large print western)
   ISBN-13: 978-1-4104-2104-3 (pbk. : alk. paper)
   ISBN-10: 1-4104-2104-X (pbk. : alk. paper)
   1. Hatfield, Jim (Fictitious character)—Fiction. 2. Texas
Rangers—Fiction. 3. Outlaws—Fiction. 4. Texas—Fiction. 5.
Large type books. I. Title.
PS3505.O2685R55 2009
813'.54—dc22   2009029884

BRITISH LIBRARY CATALOGUING-IN-PUBLICATION DATA AVAILABLE

Published in 2009 in the U.S. by arrangement with Golden West Literary Agency.
Published in 2010 in the U.K. by arrangement with Golden West Literary Agency.

U.K. Hardcover: 978 1 408 45806 8 (Chivers Large Print)
U.K. Softcover: 978 1 408 45807 5 (Camden Large Print)

Printed in the United States of America
1 2 3 4 5 6 7 13 12 11 10 09

THE SKELETON RIDERS

CHAPTER 1
GUN SCRAPES

The night wind blew across the vast Red River land of northeast Texas. It picked up grit in the streets of Sherman, flinging it against wooden walls with audible violence, stinging the faces of people outside and the hides of mustangs waiting at the hitch-rails.

Flickering lanterns served as road lamps. The town was built around a square dominated by a low, unpainted structure known as "The Court House." Stores and hotels faced this plaza and the creaking plank sidewalks were shaded by awnings. Along the ways branching off the plaza were private homes, and wagon wheel ruts crossing and crisscrossing were deeply impressed in the waxlike soil. Roughly fourteen miles to the north flowed the mighty Red. Across the stream was the wild, lawless Indian Territory, haven of killers.

The town was lively and crowded. It was a junction of many stage and freight lines.

Music and sounds of wassail rose, for at this late hour rough elements were in control, gamblers and celebrants thronging the honkytonks. Cowboys from surrounding ranches, freighters and stage drivers off the trails, travelers pausing overnight, loafers, and really dangerous customers from the brush come to town under cover of darkness rubbed elbows at the busy bars.

Abel Pyne, middle-aged, solid citizen of Sherman, started and glanced up from his newspaper. It was after eleven and he had been thinking of turning in when the sharp rap came at his door. He sat for a moment and whoever it was knocked again.

Pyne was in his bare feet, wearing comfortable old pants and a gray shirt. A six-shooter in an open holster hung by its cartridge belt from a wooden peg. He stood up, starting for the door, then on second thought turned and reached for the revolver, thrusting it into his trousers waistband before opening the door.

In the dimness on the low porch stood a stringy figure in range leather and spurred halfboots. On his head rested a flat-topped Stetson with an oval metal ornament attached to the crown, about the size and shape of a deputy's badge.

"I have an important message for Mister Abel Pyne, suh," began the visitor politely. "Is he home?"

"That's me. What's up? Do I know you?" Pyne peered at the stringy fellow, seeking to distinguish the features shadowed by the hat brim.

"Marshal Tim Suyderman told me to come, suh. Are you alone?"

"Yes, I am. Come in, come in." Pyne's caution evaporated at mention of the city marshal, an able, brave officer and an old crony of Pyne's.

The caller trailed him in and Pyne swung to stare at him in the lamplight. He had a thin, sharp face, fringed by brownish beard stubble. His protruding cheekbones were high, his muddy eyes bloodshot and sunk deeply in his bony head.

Pyne had a sudden premonition. "Say, I know you! I saw your picture on a Wanted poster at the marshal's office. You're the Wasp."

"Mister Tourneau to the likes of you, Pyne," snapped the bitter, stringy man.

Abel Pyne was an old hand. He knew he had been tricked into admitting a dangerous bandit. He made another miscalculation now, a natural one since he had no way of guessing the Wasp's real purpose. He concluded the outlaw had come to rob him and as he had his cash well-hidden and little on him, he decided to wait instead of fighting. He had a choice only for a breath for the Wasp's bony hand ripped out a Colt.

Even as Tourneau drew, a cruel grin on his facile lips, more men dashed to the veranda and bolted through the open doorway. Pyne counted a dozen in the startled glance he spared them. They wore hats of the same shape as the Wasp's, with the metal insignia. They had on masks, painted with white eyes, nose dot and grinning mouth. Above the skeleton false face their own eyes glinted. On the outsides of their boot tops were daubed white circles.

"All right, take my money," growled Pyne, raising his hands.

"I want more than that," replied Tourneau.

Then Abel Pyne realized they had come to kill him. He dropped a hand to his gun but the Wasp fired into him without further warning. A couple of Tourneau's friends threw more lead into the victim who sagged to the floor.

As the Wasp bent to check up on the dying Pyne, alarmed cries came from the street. Gunfire opened and the startled Tourneau slipped and fell flat, then rolled over gripping his pistol. Several men rushed at the outlaws, shooting and giving the shrill Rebel yell. Bullets whizzed thick through the doorway and one of Tourneau's followers, just in front of the Wasp, was hit and knocked sprawling, dead before he landed.

A plug of black chewing tobacco and a folded white paper had fallen from the Wasp's pocket as he went down but he did not notice this in the excitement. He had no time for anything but escape and scrabbled to one side, out of direct line with that door. "It's Marshal Suyderman!" shrieked a bandit, cut in the arm by a chunk of lead.

The Wasp did not delay but dove through a window, his men splitting off in all directions. A wide, heavy figure jumped inside, a man of fearless mien, bulldog jaw set. He wore a city marshal's star and worked an accurate Colt. This was Marshal Tim Suyderman, Lion of Sherman, and with him were half a dozen public-spirited and toughened citizens acting as his deputies when they were needed.

"Abel! Abel, are you bad hit? I glimpsed the Wasp and trailed him here!" Suyderman broke off with a muttered curse, realizing that his friend was past hearing anything. "Come on, boys, after the sidewinders!"

11

They ran out in pursuit and guns barked in Sherman as they sought to bring down more of the skeleton-masked killers.

Young Lake Staples yawned and shifted his position a bit to ease his muscles. He was standing night guard for his employer, Lucius Evans, owner of the Box E Ranch which was northward of Sherman, Texas. Sherman was nearly ten miles away while the Red River ran four miles above the rise on which the buildings stood. A tributary of the mighty Red furnished the cattle and the people with water.

The moon was full and high in the sky and Staples could pick out details by its brilliance. The long, low house, made of rough lumber cut at a sawmill after being hauled from the forest, stood against the silver sky, powdered with pale stars. A barn, small bunkhouse, a couple of sheds and cribs, corrals with rail shadows distinctly black on the lighter ground, flat wagons and equipment showed at the Box E headquarters.

Slowly, Lake Staples rounded the barn to start another tour, stepping into the bright moonlight. He carried a loaded rifle and in his side holster rode a six-shooter. Whipcord riding pants and spurred halfboots adorned his sturdy legs. His shirt was brown and he had pushed up the brim of his high Stetson in front. He was in his early twenties, tireless and good-natured. His powerful body was well-formed, his flesh bronzed and his blue eyes clear and steady on the beholder, his features as even as his temper.

Staples was a typical Texas cowboy. His mother had died when he was a small child and he had run away from home at the age of fourteen to ride the range. After difficult years of knocking around he had grown to full size and had made several trips up the Trail to Kansas with Lone Star herds. A couple of years before he had stopped at the Box E and Evans had taken him on as a hand. Staples had remained at the ranch because of Edith Evans, daughter of the house. Edith was a couple of years younger than he, an animated, chestnut-haired beauty.

The young woman was asleep inside now and besides guarding the woman he loved, Lake Staples had a deep sense of duty to his employer and to the Evans family. He was deeply attached to them all and willing to sacrifice his own life for them if need be.

The threat to the Box E was somewhat vague. Several days before a letter had been delivered by messenger from Sherman. The settlement, which was an important crossroads for stage and freight lines, was the bailiwick of Marshal Tim Suyderman, a courageous officer who had been bracing the outlaws from Indian Territory. Suyderman warned Evans, an old friend, that the rancher's life was in danger. The marshal had mentioned Ed Tourneau, the Wasp, a dangerous bandit chief infesting north Texas. Abel Pyne, a decent citizen of Sherman, had already been slain. But Suyderman could furnish no logical reason, beyond ordinary robbery, as to why the Wasp had been ordered to slay Abel Pyne and others, among them Evans and two Box E neighbors, George Welder of the 1–2 and Duncan Kilgore of the Slash K, who shared common range in the vicinity.

Lucius Evans had not been unduly alarmed at the threat to his life. He was a Confederate veteran and had fought in the Texas brigades throughout the terrible conflict. He had pioneered in the Red River land, fighting Indians and worse white outlaws and had raised a family and held his own. Such men were not easily stampeded; in fact, they were apt to pooh-pooh danger and be over-confident. But Mrs. Evans and Edith had insisted some consideration be given to Suyderman's warning. Hence, a waddy had been posted on night guard. Nothing had occurred and the ranch had relaxed.

"Buffalo gals, are you comin' out tonight, comin' out tonight, comin' out tonight — dance by the light of the moon!" Staples hummed the familiar tune in a low voice so as not to disturb anybody. The night was warm, windows and doors stood wide open. In the main house slept the family, in the bunkhouse his comrades, waddies of the Box E.

Suddenly Staples checked his slow patrol, listening with cocked head. Then he ran around to the north side of the ranch. Across a rolling plain which led to the banks of the mighty Red, drove a welter of horsemen. The beat of the numerous hoofs had telegraphed through the earth and warned Lake Staples of their approach.

Their speed brought them swiftly in. In the moonlight, Staples made out their dark figures but what was really startling were their faces. Every one had whitened eyes, nose and grinning mouth slash and at a couple of hundred yards the face seemed that of a skeleton. The astonished Staples lost another couple of seconds as he stared, the strange uniformity of their countenances puzzling him.

Then he uttered a double-sized whoop

and fired his rifle over the oncoming riders. "Box E, up and at 'em! All out, here they come!" A volley roared his way. He saw the flaming muzzles and hastily skipped around the turn as bullets rapped into the wooden wall or kicked up dirt spurts at its base.

Staples crouched at the corner, calling to his friends. There was no doubt as to the intention of the approaching band. Marshal Suyderman had been right. Staples peered out, and as the enemy had rapidly drawn closer he could distinguish more details. Over glowing silver-white round orbs glinted a second pair of eyes, a bizarre impression. "Masks!" muttered the cowboy. White paint daubs on dark cloth formed the mask each killer wore. All seemed to have on flat-topped hats, in front a shining metal ornament.

Staples could see white circles painted on boot tops pressed against the heaving mustang ribs.

Already the ranch, alerted by the guard's shouts, had jumped to action. At Evans' order, they had slept on their arms and all a man had to do was leap up, seize his gun and rush forth to battle. Lake Staples aimed his second shot and hit a horse which slew off and threw its rider. On the next squeeze of his trigger, Staples got the dismounted bandit. Rifles began flashing from the house windows and a knot of cowboys from the bunkhouse trotted into position, squatting in the shadows and throwing lead at the attackers.

Staples could see what was going to happen and he swung, dove through an open window and took up his position there. Met by a hot fusillade, the outlaws howled like coyotes and the driving band split against the house, veering to either side and shooting from their saddles as they passed.

Lake managed to wound another as they flew by his loophole. Then they had spurred on and out of easy range, pulled rein and swung to reform.

"Hair in the butter! What in tarnation blazes is all this about?" boomed a deep commanding voice in the brief lull. "Lake, where are you? You hit?"

"No suh. They were comin' like the heel flies were after 'em, suh, and I barely had time to signal," replied Staples, rising to join his boss, Lucius Evans of the Box E.

"Edie, light a candle but keep it shaded," ordered Evans. "Jeff, break out that extra carbine ammunition, pronto, hop to it. Mike, tell the boys to come in, we'll hold the house if nothin' else. Why, the cusses brought an army along to wipe us up!"

The dim flicker of a match, then the tiny yellow flame of a candle offered a bit of illumination. Lucius Evans was a tall, powerful Texan, his goatee and mustache, his thick curly hair, touched by gray. Once a Confederate officer of cavalry, his wind-browned hide had a reddish tinge, and his dark eyes were strong. His nose had a high ridge, hooked like a hawk's beak. He had on gray pants and shirt and had run out in his bare feet at the alarm.

Edith Evans, daughter of the household, was a chestnut-haired beauty, with an oval, animated face and mischievous amber eyes. She was small, beautifully formed, and she glanced at Lake Staples first of all to make sure he was not hurt. Her mother, Flora, had joined the group in the main room, a comely woman from whom Edith had inherited her good looks. The three sons, Mike, Jeff and Wash, were strapping young fellows, Mike, the eldest, having just turned twenty, and Wash, the baby, being sixteen. Mike now returned, leading half a dozen armed cowboys who worked for Evans. They had been asleep in the bunkhouse when the attack opened.

Jeff fetched in two gunnysacks from a storeroom and cut the drawstrings, dumping cartridges in a heap on the mat. "Help yourselves, boys," said Evans. "Pick a loop and keep to one side, don't show yourselves like danged fools. They outnumber us five to one."

Doors were bolted and heavy pieces of furniture shoved against them. An inverted bushel basket was placed over the candle for they needed a bit of light by which to load and move about. Edith and her mother would tend guns and give a hand, and when a fighter was wounded, the women would attend to him.

Wash Evans, who had been peeking from a window on the other side, called a warning. "Here they come back, Pop!"

"Keep low, folks," warned Lucius Evans. He had his pet rifle snugged to his shoulder as he knelt by a window corner, off at an angle so bullets tearing through would not easily find him. The ranchers roared a challenge at the marauders. "What you sidewinders want here? Move off or we'll cut you down!"

A sharp voice answered. "Surrender, Evans. If you show any more fight, not one of you will find any mercy in us."

Staples was at the window next to the one covered by his employer. He took careful aim with his carbine as lines of skeleton-faced horsemen savagely spurted at the Box E.

CHAPTER 2
ORDERED TO DANGER

Captain William McDowell, chief of Texas Rangers at Austin, hunched over his desk, staring at the strange letter clutched in his gnarled hand. Mellow sunshine stole through the windows at headquarters but nature's blandishment could not soothe the ancient officer. He was seething with volcanic wrath.

A fighting man from all the way back, Bill McDowell had been pinned down by the infirmities of age. Yet he was still indispensable to his mighty state in the endless struggle between good and evil. Texas was huge and offered so many tempting opportunities to outlaw minds that the handful of hard-pressed field operatives available had to keep eternally on the move. "Hatfield's just come in from a tough job. He ought to have a breather but this is so all-fired important I'll have to send him out pronto," muttered McDowell. He banged the call-bell and gave his orders, jumping to his feet and pacing back and forth as he waited.

An astonishingly large, powerful young man soon slouched into the sanctum. This was Jim Hatfield, McDowell's best officer. He stood well over six feet, his deep chest and wide shoulders tapering to a slim waist, ringed by belts from which depended the oiled holsters casing his heavy Colt revolvers. The legerdemain speed with which Hatfield could bring his guns into play was known to the old captain. Hatfield could fight with a panther's ruthless savagery against evil antagonists. He could outlast any man in the saddle and in withstanding hardships in the field.

"Yes suh, Cap'n Bill," drawled Hatfield. His voice was soft, and very gentle. Slim hands hung easily at his sides. He wore no uniform, his clothing that of the range rider, leather trousers, a blue shirt, a big Stetson, bandanna, spurred riding boots. Long lashes shaded his gray-green eyes, the tight jaw and lean face broken by a wide, good-natured mouth. His black hair was crisp with youthful health.

Beyond his physical attributes, Hatfield had that intangible characteristic which made him a leader among men and drew others to him. People felt his strength and took comfort in it. He could think quickly and accurately in the teeth of danger. For in the struggles he waged, more than sheer smashing force had to be used. His mind was brilliant, capable of coping with the shrewd, devious machinations of the super outlaws he had to brace.

"This is the brazenest yet!" growled McDowell. "Look at this. In all my years buckin' bandits, I never saw anything like it." He shoved the letter toward the Ranger. "Marshal Tim Suyderman of Sherman, up on the Red River, sent it to me."

The grave, gray-green eyes scanned the bold, flowing script.

Dispose at once of the following: Abel Pyne, who lives in the square white house on North Main. Lucius Evans, owner of the Box E north of Sherman, George Welder of the 1–2 and Duncan Kilgore, Slash K. By now you must have organized according to my instructions. I want disciplined men and the methods I ordered are best. Make no errors. This is vital. Will join you on the 12th.

There was neither salutation nor signature.

23

"Where did Marshal Suyderman get this, suh?" asked Hatfield.

"He found it close to Abel Pyne's body in Sherman. They have already tried for ranchers mentioned and by this time may have succeeded in finishin' 'em. You can trust Suyderman, he's a good hombre and an unusually fine officer for a town marshal. He'll give the Rangers all possible assistance. Here's Suyderman's note, which came with that outlaw letter. The marshal says he spotted an outlaw chief named Ed Tourneau, known as the Wasp, at Pyne's the night Pyne was shot. The Wasp hides out in the Territory and commands a bunch of gunhands."

Jim Hatfield nodded. "We've had plenty trouble up that way, suh, and we'll go on havin' it till Indian Territory is settled and under real law. Every killer and bandit in the country heads for it to hide out."

He rose to take his leave as McDowell finished briefing him. In the sun-kissed yard, a beautiful golden gelding awaited the Ranger. The sorrel was a magnificent animal, capable of carrying the tall officer on his perilous, hard-driving missions. Beside the excellent saddle, there was a carbine in its boot, a slicker roll at the cantle, while Goldy's saddle pockets contained iron rations and a few necessities for life in the field.

Hatfield swung a long leg over his hull, waved to the Captain, watching with nostalgic longing as the Ranger set forth.

The Ranger's first stop was at a neat cottage on the outskirts of the capital. Westward, Mount Bonnell loomed over the flowing blue Colorado.

Austin, heart of Texas, was built on wide terraces stepping back from the river banks.

A lean youth of around sixteen rushed out to greet Hatfield. "Jim! Will you take me along this trip?"

"I reckon so, Buck, if your sister can spare you."

"Buck" Robertson was his protégé. The sun had bleached his light hair a tow color, his face was freckled, his nose tilted up. He was still growing, his lean figure in levis and a gray shirt. Hatfield was teaching him Ranger ways. The lad had a daring disposition and he needed the guidance and example of a strong man. Whenever he could, Hatfield took Buck along on his field runs, for the work served as an outlet for Buck's bubbling energy, and often he proved of use to the officer.

Anita, Buck's sister, came to smile up at Hatfield. She was a shapely young woman, a schoolma'am by profession. The light glinted on her golden hair, neatly arranged on her trim head. "Yes, surely, Buck may go," she agreed.

With a whoop of joy, Buck dashed toward the stable behind the cottage to saddle Old Heart 7, his chunky gray mustang. Hatfield spoke with Anita as he waited for his companion to make ready. The Ranger had come to the assistance of the Robertsons on the Brazos when they had been in peril, and they had become fast friends.

She stood on the lawn, waving to them as they rode away. The Red River was a long, arduous journey from Austin.

On the highway, as they neared Sherman, they had passed immense wagon trains carrying merchandise, creaking forward with great wheels caked by waxy soil. Night was at hand and in the warmth a haze hung over the seemingly unlimited range, rolling on and on, broken here and there by stands of timber or the upthrusts of great rock formations.

The lights were on as they walked their horses through the outskirts of Sherman, to the public square in the heart of the settlement. John Butterfield had been persuaded to route the St. Louis to San Francisco stage line through the town and this had assured Sherman's growth as a marketing and transportation center, stages and freight wagons heading for the junction.

The plaza was spacious, with large, substantial buildings surrounding the square. Stores and saloons were abundant. Horsemen and citizens on foot showed in the yellow glow by oil-burning street lamps. Sherman was the county seat and the low, unpainted wooden Court House stood in the center. Saddled mustangs and mules awaited their masters, reins over the numerous rails. The plank sidewalks were crowded and Sherman was humming as usual.

Dubious looking characters rubbed elbows with spruce speculators from north and west, and in the middle of things, dogs and swine trotted hither and yon, picking up scraps and enjoying the company. There were plenty of loafers lounging on wooden benches along the walls. Music issued from honkytonks, the shrill voices of women joining with the cries of drunken men. Travelers, stopping overnight in Sherman, were out sightseeing before turning in at the hotel.

"We'll snatch a bite and then we'll contact Marshal Tim Suyderman, Buck," said Ranger Hatfield. "It's dark and we can see him without all the rascals in town knowin' we're here."

There were plenty of places to buy a meal and the two stoked up with appetites keened by long hours of riding since the last mouthful. The Court House was dark. One door was marked "City Marshal" outside but it was locked.

"Tell you what," ordered Hatfield. "You go ask the bartender over there where Suyderman lives. He may be on patrol or he could be home eatin' before the town tunes up for the evenin'."

Buck soon rejoined him. Suyderman lived in a small cabin up the next side street, according to Buck's information, and the two mounted and headed for it. They swung off the main stem into a narrow byway. Rays from windows slanted across the rutted road while here and there a lantern was strung on a post. By this light they could distinguish details. Buck pointed at a one-room shack set back a few paces from the plank sidewalk to their right.

"That's it for shore, Jim. The barkeep said we couldn't miss it."

"Push to the side. Let all those riders go by," ordered the Ranger. From the opposite direction bunches of horsemen came through the street.

Hatfield and Buck drew close to the walk but the band pulled rein and turned in, facing toward Suyderman's. The Ranger noted a metal ornament attached to the flat-topped Stetson worn by each rider and at first impression thought these fellows might be deputies. "Looks like they're collectin' for posse work at the marshal's," he murmured.

A couple of leaders jumped down. "Marshal Suyderman! Hustle, there's a killin' up the road!" shouted one, in an excited voice.

The Ranger uttered a startled exclamation. The armed crew pulled up masks which had been looped about their throats, ready to be raised. He stared at the strange features, grinning, oversized mouth, daubed nose and round white orbs, while above the latter a second pair of eyes showed, offering a bizarre impression. To an unfortunate victim the aspect of the attackers could be most terrifying.

Hatfield reached for a Colt, the hammer spur under a long thumb as the weapon cleared the oiled, supple leather case. "Watch it, Buck! I don't like the looks of this."

They had been seen and several masked men trotted their horses at the two, pushed them to the edge of the street. "Go on, dust out of here if you know what's good for you!" sang out the fellow in front. Hatfield could make out their dark figures, and their guns were rising.

"Douse your light and stay inside, Suyderman!" bellowed the Ranger, throwing a quickie over the array of skeleton-faced gunhands.

But the cabin door was already opening. In the yellow rectangle appeared a wide, heavy figure. Hatfield had an impression of a bulldog face and the gleam of a bald pate but then a dozen Colts and shotguns roared in unison. The man in the doorway was hit by a shower of bullets, shuddering as the murderous metal drove into him. The pistol he had in one hand rose and flamed, a final defiance, but he was sagging and fell on his doorsill, the attackers pouring more and more lead into the body.

"He's done in," gasped Buck.

"Let's get out of here. Nothin' we can do now."

Weapons were rising and shots answered the Ranger's Colt. Metal rapped into the house walls or kicked splinters from the plank sidewalk as they spurred off and picking up speed, drove for the turn. Hoarse yells, threatening them for their interference in the marshal's behalf, reached their ears as they sped for safety, low over their horses. The whole band, with Suyderman killed, turned on the pair.

Chapter 3
Broken Contact

Bullets were hunting Buck and the Ranger but before the masked killers could bring their concerted fire around to riddle the fast-moving targets they had reached the corner, jerking rein and sliding around it into the square.

"They're comin' for us," said the Ranger. "Put the Court House between your hide and the cusses, Buck. Pronto."

In spite of the crowds, alarmed at the bursts of gunfire from the side way, the marauders dug in their spurs, whooping it up like coyotes as they followed Hatfield and his youthful comrade. Men jumped back for shelter, hunting cover, while the loafers disappeared as though by magic. In Sherman, as in most frontier settlements, it was every man for himself and nobody cared to interfere in a stranger's behalf at the cost of his own life. Boldly, the galloping outlaws surged into the plaza and pelted on the Ranger's trail. Slugs hunted the two who turned behind the bulky Court House.

"Come on, get Old Heart 7 movin'," ordered Hatfield, kicking the chunky gray mustang ahead. He took the rear guard, Colt gripped in one hand, guiding with his knees as he glanced back. His chinstrap was taut, the rugged jaw set and his gray-green eyes had darkened, icy as an Arctic sea.

As they hastily left the Court House they were again visible to the pursuers. But they made for a street leading westward, and aware of singing lead over them and around their galloping mounts, cut between two lines of houses. Goldy and Old Heart 7 were superior animals and good for a fast spurt, though they had come a long way that afternoon.

For a time it was a race. They tore over a rolling, moonlit flat, the top of the ridge on which Sherman was built. As they left the town behind them, the rank and file of the masked gunslingers fell hopelessly to the rear, a few keeping up the chase for a quarter mile before they sent a last, futile burst after the two out front.

Southwest, a patch of timber, below the dropping slope, drew Hatfield and Buck. They reached the dark shadows and pulled up for a breather. Reconnoitering, they found that the pursuers had given it up as a bad job and were moving northward, either returning to Sherman or headed for the Red River.

Hatfield removed his Stetson to mop his brow. "I'm afeared that was Marshal Suyderman they downed, Buck. That cuts our contact here. I was shore countin' on him. They say he was a real brave officer."

"If we'd have got there a mite sooner, folks could say the same for you, Jim," remarked Buck gravely. "They'd have caught us in there, off our guard."

They waited, resting their horses for an hour, then mounted and returned to Sherman, taking care to enter from another direction. But the center was normal enough and they saw no sign of their enemies. Hatfield entered a large honkytonk and soon was engaged in conversation with a friendly bartender. Such gentry were sources of local information.

"Yes suh," the barkeeper told him cheerily. "They shore finished pore Tim Suyderman. He had twenty bullets in him, they say. Well, that Wasp and his bunch are mighty tough. I don't aim to tangle with 'em, not for all the gold in Californy."

"So you figger it was the Wasp plugged the marshal?"

The bartender shrugged and wiped the counter with a damp cloth. "Who else? Suyderman's been after Tourneau for a long while, and this ain't the first scrap they've had, though I reckon it's the last. Old Tim was a good feller."

"I'd like a peek at this Wasp hombre. Could you point him out?"

"Oh, he ain't here now. He only comes to town now and again. Those fellers hide out across the Red, in I.T."

The Ranger's silver star on silver circle, emblem of his office, was snugged in a secret pocket inside his shirt. It was his habit to enter a case without fanfare and learn the details of a situation before publicly announcing his identity. To the observer he looked like a big cowhand or rancher, and could pass as such.

Hatfield rejoined Buck, who was on watch near the entry. He pointed out the bartender with whom he had been conversing. "You can spiel with him, Buck. We've lost our local contact in Sherman, with the marshal dead. I want to call on Lucius Evans at the Box E and mebbe he can tell me somethin'. I hope that ravenin' bunch of four-eyed rascals hasn't overrun him yet."

They rode to a nearby livery stable, open

all night, unsaddled the horses and rubbed them down, seeing to the animals themselves. Goldy and the chunky gray were left in a corral behind the stable while Hatfield and Buck rented a room at a hotel and turned in, weary from their exertions.

In the morning they consumed a hearty breakfast. Hatfield fixed a quirly and they stood leaning against a wooden wall, watching the bustling square, the Ranger giving his youthful friend instructions. "I'm ridin' to the Box E to see Evans, Buck; it's near ten miles north and a bit east of here, I understand. You stick in town and watch for the Wasp. With the marshal out of it, that letter is all I got to go on."

Glorious sunshine bathed Sherman. The plank sidewalks were crammed with men, some in patched homespun, others in dandy's attire, with women in bustled dresses and bonnets. Saddle horses and teams stood thick in the plaza. Travelers were coming out to embark in the stages, drawn by plunging mules or horses, the drivers swearing and plying the whip. Swine rooted in the streets, picking up garbage flung from doors and windows, lean hounds were snarling and fighting over scraps of meat.

Big freight wagons were loading or unloading down the line and across the way

an auctioneer with a voice as shrilly pen-
etrating as a whistle blast was selling off
bales of cotton. Fierce looking riders, rifle
slung over shoulder, saddlebags stuffed with
game, cantered by on spirited mustangs,
some leading pack mules with deer or buffalo quarters as loads, hunters off the plains
come to sell their produce.

As the Ranger and Buck watched, a slow
moving flat wagon appeared from the lane
on which Suyderman had lived. It carried a
plain pine box and there were several
mourners along. "There goes the last of a
brave hombre," growled Hatfield, touching
the brim of his Stetson. "The Wasp will pay
for that."

He felt that Buck would be safe enough
around Sherman so long as the youth did
not attempt anything foolhardy. The masked
killers could scarcely have distinguished
their features or much about them during
that swift brush of the previous evening.

"Lie low, Buck, and keep your eye peeled,"
warned Hatfield. "Don't hunt any scrapes."

Buck accompanied him to the livery stable
where Hatfield saddled the golden sorrel.
Taking leave of his comrade, the Ranger
rode through town and hit a winding track
leading roughly northward, in which direction lay the Red River. About fifteen miles

from the ridge on which Sherman was situated a ferry crossed the stream. Below the Red and east along its uneven margin was the cattle range, the river serving as a drift fence for the pastures. Evans' home was two thirds of the run to the ferry.

A brand sign nailed on a post had directed Jim Hatfield off the road. He crossed a shallow creek and sighted low buildings, a long house of weathered lumber, a barn and small bunkhouse, cribs, corrals with mustangs standing around. He had seen bunches of cows grazing as he approached.

The sun was yellow and warm and the spot seemed peacefully pastoral. The side creek was a tributary of the Red, winding this way and that, its banks lined with willows, alders and scrub growth.

The Ranger stared at the Box E. Nobody seemed to be around and this worried him. Possibly the Wasp had already struck with all his force. Then a faint puff of warm wind brought the odors of frying beef and of coffee coming to a boil. As he rode a bit closer he could make out the hot vapor issuing from a chimney, though the wood fire had burned to smokeless embers in the stove. He kept going and drew up in the yard.

"What you want?" challenged a hard voice.

Hatfield glanced around and saw a rifle muzzle, covering him from a barn window.

"Hold it," called Hatfield. "I'm a cattle buyer from Waco. Is Mister Evans around?" Even if by chance the enemy had taken the ranch, this identification would not betray him.

A deeper, commanding voice spoke to him from the house. "Light and set. If you're what you say, you won't be hurt, suh. Come over to the front porch and let's have a good look at you."

Hatfield got down and taking care to keep his moves deliberate, strode to the low veranda. The door was open and he stood there, aware those inside were inspecting him and had him covered. The guard from the barn had emerged and was crossing the yard, rifle up, finger on trigger. The waddy was a young, well-made man, bronze of flesh, his blue eyes keen and steady.

He wore range clothes, the brim of his Stetson turned up above his clean face. As he came into position so he could watch the visitor from the rear, a tall, powerful Texan of middle age came out of the house to confront the Ranger. His head was bare, his lion mane of curly hair, the goatee and mustache, touched by silver. He had a high-bridged hawk nose, and flashing dark eyes, and wore gray trousers and a faded shirt of the same hue. A heavy pistol was thrust into his black belt.

"Are you Mister Lucius Evans, suh?" asked the Ranger politely.

"I might be. Who are you and what's your business? Do you wish to buy cattle?"

Hatfield gave a brief shake of his head. Evans was staring up at him, impressed by his size and obvious power. "I'm from Austin, suh." He was sure of the rancher now, he could read honesty and good-heartedness in the strong man before him. And past Evans, he had seen younger men, slim and with their father's cast of visage, undoubtedly sons of the household, and a pretty young woman standing by a table set for the noon meal.

Before coming close to the Box E, Jim Hatfield had extracted his badge and he held it in his left hand. Now he opened his fingers so Lucius Evans could see the silver star on silver circle. The rancher's manner immediately relaxed and he grinned. "Texas Ranger! Come in, suh, please do. Mighty glad you're here. If you'll be so kind, maybe you'll sample some of Mother's cookin'."

He sang out to the sturdy sentinel. "All right, Lake, this hombre is a friend. Shorty

40

fed early. Tell him to take over and you eat with us yore-ownself."

"My handle is Jim Hatfield, Mister Evans. I'd as soon not let too many folks savvy I'm a Ranger, till I've looked around."

"I savvy. We'll keep it close. That's Lake Staples, my best rider. You can ride the river with him any time. But come in, come in."

Hatfield entered the spacious main room. Introductions were in order. Hatfield's eye was taken by the chestnut-haired beauty, small and beautifully formed, who demurely greeted him as her father introduced her as his daughter Edith. She curtseyed, and he thought he detected amusement in her eyes. Mrs. Evans was comely, smiling and hospitable.

"My sons, Mike, Jeff and Wash," went on Evans, indicating the three strapping young fellows in leather.

Wash was about Buck's age. They stepped down a couple of inches in height from Mike, the eldest, with a strong brotherly resemblance.

"None of my boys have been sent to jail or elected to the legislature," jested their father. "I think that's a pretty good showin'."

At the side of the room waited a stout man, with a thick mustache and wide-set blue eyes fixed on the newcomer. He wore black trousers tucked into spurred calfskin boots, blue shirt and vest. His hair was thinning on top. He was perhaps four or five years younger than Lucius Evans. "This is George Welder, my neighbor on the east, Mister Hatfield. He owns the 1–2 Ranch." Welder shook hands, sun-seamed eyes smiling. The Ranger sized him up, for Welder was another of the victims itemized in the letter sent to McDowell by Marshal Suyderman.

Lake Staples came in the back way, removed his Stetson and stood near Edith, on whose finger Hatfield saw a gold ring. The Ranger decided from the young couple's manner that they were in love.

Dinner was ready, the board loaded with tempting viands. They sat down and the tall officer enjoyed home-made bread and butter, roast beef, preserves, good coffee and other delicacies. The Evans women obviously were excellent cooks. While they ate, Lucius Evans and Welder told the guest about the attacks which had been made upon them by the enemy.

"They wear masks painted with skeleton faces," Welder said. "The cusses came for me one night, but we beat 'em off. That was after they hit Evans and we were ready for 'em."

"How about Duncan Kilgore, Slash K?" inquired Hatfield.

"He ain't been attacked yet, but he's expectin' it. His spread is about five miles southeast of us," replied Lucius Evans.

The officer listened to the ranchers' accounts, weighing what they told him. They did not understand why Abel Pyne, who had been a decent, fine citizen, had been rudely slain by the Wasp and his crew, nor why they were being subjected to the vicious persecution of the outlaws. A Box E cowboy had been in Sherman early that morning to buy supplies and had returned with the shocking news of Marshal Suyderman's killing. The local officer's loss was a sad blow to the cowmen.

Hatfield brought forth the stained letter which had been picked up by Suyderman near Abel Pyne's body. Evans nodded as he saw it. "The marshal showed it to us before sendin' it to Austin, suh."

"You don't know who might have written these orders to Tourneau?"

Welder and Evans shook their heads. The Wasp's chief was unknown to them.

After the pleasing, substantial meal, the two ranchers and the Ranger sat smoking on the porch for a time, talking of plans to

43

combat the foe. Then George Welder took his leave, starting back to his home. Hatfield thought he would like to meet Duncan Kilgore, the third involved in the letter.

"Staples will ride over with you," said Evans. "Dunc's on guard just like we are."

During the run, Hatfield talked with the cowboy. Staples was bright and very good-natured. He had an understanding with Edith Evans, as Hatfield had guessed, and by the time they arrived at the Slash K, a small ranch also on guard against the Wasp, the Ranger knew all about his companion, that Staples was a strong, splendid young fellow and worthy of the recommendation given by his employer.

Staples eased the way for him as they dismounted at the Slash K, introducing Jim Hatfield to Duncan Kilgore, a slim, wiry man with a black ribbon mustache and thin beard. Kilgore was of Scotch descent, dour, solemn, but upright and honest. For a time the Ranger chatted with him but Kilgore could add nothing to what the others had told the officer from Austin.

"Stay on guard, suh, and I'll see what's what," advised Hatfield as he said good-bye. "You'll hear from me soon."

He dropped Lake Staples at the Box E, rested and watered Goldy, then started his return to Sherman, taking a roundabout route so he could get a better idea of the country. Ridges rose, step on step, back from the wide valley of the Red, over which hung a pastel haze. The grass was good. Patches of woods and the winding lines of brooks and creeks, broke the land. The Ranger knew there was a ferry to take passengers from Texas to Indian Territory at the end of the road between Sherman and the river. Cattle herds and mustang bands, being driven to Kansas and other northern markets, passed not far westward. Travelers on horseback moved back and forth across the Territory, at their peril.

Night had fallen as he rode back into Sherman. Buck Robertson was watching for him, waiting near the livery stable. "The Wasp's in town, Jim! He pulled up half an hour ago and went into the Ace Hotel."

"Is he still here, you reckon?"

"I think so. I kept an eye on him and after a couple of drinks in the bar, he went up to a second-floor rear room. There's armed guards on duty so I hustled here, hopin' you'd show. It's Room Sixteen."

"Bueno. You're shore it's our man?"

"Positive. I made friends with a feller my age who polishes boots in the plaza. He pointed out Tourneau, the Wasp, a stringy,

45

mean lookin' cuss."

"Good work, Buck. We'll see what we can see."

Goldy cared for, the tall officer from Austin moved toward the noisy honkytonk occupying the northeast corner of the square. From Buck's report it sounded as though Ed Tourneau, field chief of the skeleton riders, was making a business contact. Hatfield was hoping for just this since the letter proved that the Wasp took orders from someone above.

CHAPTER 4
HIDEOUT

Buck pointed at a long-legged, saffron-hided horse, with a silver-inlaid saddle cinched on its back. The animal was a fine one, the hull worth hundreds of dollars.

"That's the Wasp's bronc, Jim, so he ain't left yet. I hope none of 'em remember us from that little set-to."

"It isn't likely. Stick outside and watch."

Hatfield entered the saloon. The bar was long, and beside the dance floor were tables at which patrons might drink and eat. Attached wings held gaming parlors where every type of device was used to separate players from their cash. Poker and roulette, dice and birdcage, were running wide open as the Ranger looked around. The click of wheels, the babble, stamping feet as men jigged about with dancing women to the tunes blared out by piano and fiddles, made an ear-filling din. Customers stood three-deep at the bar. Some had white circles daubed on their boot uppers and were wearing flat-crowned hats with the nickel insignia in front. He was sure these were some of the Wasp's followers. As none paid him any special attention, he felt safe in concluding they did not recognize the elusive fugitive they had gone for after killing Marshal Suyderman.

The saloon was part of the Ace hotel. Guests were in the lobby and on the stairs. The Ranger strolled through and paused at the call desk, leaning on an elbow. A clerk stood nearby, on the counter a large, open ledger served as a register. "Howdy, suh," said Hatfield politely. "Is Room Sixteen taken?"

"Yes, mister. Professor Brite holds it for when he's in town. Fact is, we got no vacancies tonight, but we could bed you down in the stable."

"Well, I'll see about that later. Did you say Professor Brite? I wonder if he's the hombre of the same name that I know. Where's he hail from? Did he register?"

"Oh yes. Everybody has to sign. Here he is." The clerk was friendly enough with the tall man, who had a knack for making people like him. He pointed to a signature so Hatfield could see for himself.

Hatfield showed no sign of elation but the

handwriting indicated matched that of the letter sent to the Wasp. "Professor Leming Brite, New Orleans, La." Under this was a cramped signature, "George Karnes," a ditto mark beneath New Orleans. The Ranger chatted for a time. "Reckon I'll step up and see if it's my pard, suh. He was from Galveston but he might have moved to New Orleans."

The clerk nodded and turned to another customer, having no objection as Hatfield climbed the stairs. He found himself in a hall running from back to front. To his left was a longer corridor in which, close to the farther end, slouched three gunhands wearing flat Stetsons, their waists circled by cartridge belts. He concluded they must be the guard outside the room into which Ed Tourneau had gone. As they casually glanced his way, he walked straight on, room doors on both sides, and soon came to the hall serving rooms overlooking the square. This way was parallel to the rear aisle, and he moved along to the fourth side of the rectangle, similar to the first but with no stairs leading up to it.

He stepped softly since the construction was very flimsy. Cracks yawned between upright, unpainted boards serving as partitions, the raw lumber having shrunk

49

throughout the years. The rooms on the inner section would have no windows, only skylights, though not much space was wasted. Obviously the extra story had been hastily added, no doubt to accommodate the flood of travelers arriving when Sherman had become a junction.

The hotel shook from the stamping below, the din rising with little hindrance. What slight sounds the Ranger made were lost in the shuffle, the hum of voices and clinking of glass, the sentries chatting and drinking just around the corner.

At the turns the wall space was twice that between the other rooms. He wondered if a single door might serve two-room suites and decided to find out. The last door in his corridor was just out of sight of the guards. He stopped there, listening but could catch no hint there might be occupants inside. The tenants, at such an early hour, would no doubt be downstairs or out somewhere, eating and drinking. Hatfield tried the latch. It lifted and the thin panel pushed open.

The room was dark save for what little light slanted in from the windows, open on a side court. As he entered, he was not challenged, and he closed the door, found the bolt and shot it home. He could see two cots, a bureau, chairs and other furnishings around. And as he had hoped, there was a connection into the corner room which did not have a hall entry.

As he tiptoed across the second chamber he saw faint yellow slits of light coming between the cracks. He was next to Room Sixteen, and lost no time in placing an eye to one of the narrow openings.

Three men sat in there, conferring over a bottle of whiskey. Blue smoke from their cheroots curled around a hanging gilt lamp. On the cots lay a couple of satchels. One of the talkers was Ed Tourneau, the Wasp, a stringy man with yellowish skin and a thin face, his mouth bitterly lined. Buck, Staples and others had amply described Tourneau. Because of the hubbub from below it was difficult to catch much of what was being said, but after a time the Ranger was sure that the Wasp addressed one of his companions as "Professor."

He studied the fellow carefully. Leming Brite was long and lanky, with broad shoulders filling his silk shirt. Striped trousers were fastened under his long-toed boots by elastic loops. On a bed, by a satchel, lay a frock coat and shining high hat which must be the Professor's. Brite's hair was coal-black and gleamed in the lamplight, every strand pomaded in place. This growth was most luxuriant and parted in the middle with mathematical precision.

His high-boned face was lengthened by combed dark sideburns, his mouth a determined one, the nose predatory. He shifted restlessly and Hatfield glimpsed the black handle of a six-shooter thrust into Brite's belt. A long foot tapped the floor, and Brite opened his thin lips and clicked his teeth. His eyes were round and bright as shoe-buttons and the pun instantly occurred to the spying Ranger. "Bright Eyes, shore enough," he thought.

The Professor reached in a shirt pocket and brought forth a flat silver box. He clicked this open and in a most gentlemanly fashion took a pinch of snuff between bony forefinger and thumb, sniffed it, and used a large kerchief in which to sneeze. All in all, Brite's manner was elegant and most superior.

But the conference, to Hatfield's disappointment, was about over. Brite stood up, nodding. "See you in the morning. Need sleep."

Hatfield decided that the third man must be George Karnes, who had checked in with Professor Leming Brite. Karnes was oversized, powerful in build. His light hair was clipped short on his round head, his eyes a pale-blue. He wore a white shirt and blue trousers and a pistol in a shoulder holster whose strap crossed his mighty chest. In some long ago brawl his nose had been mashed in and this, added to a cauliflower ear, did not improve his features. Karnes looked really tough.

"Come on, Brakeman, I'll show you the town," said the Wasp, rising.

Brakeman Karnes seized his black hat and set it on his head. From the pocket of a blue coat, lying near his suitcase on the bed, he brought forth a steel spanner, a long wrench such as railroaders use in their work. He flourished this at the Wasp, grinning on one side of his thick-lipped mouth. "Persuader," he announced, and dropped the spanner into his pants pocket.

Ed Tourneau and Brakeman Karnes saluted Brite. They closed the door as they left. The Professor took a document from his satchel and for a time studied it under the hanging lamp, hunched over the table. From a neat round leather case he extracted a bottle of ink and a pen, and made a few improvements or changes. Replacing the paper, he unfolded another, larger paper which the watching Ranger thought might be a map. Once, as he worked, Brite turned around and stared straight at the wall and it seemed to Hatfield the Professor must have heard him, perhaps glimpsed the sheen of his gray-green eye pressed to the crack.

But then Brite lighted a cheroot, and carefully put away his work. He threw down a couple of stiff jolts of redeye and smoked away. Soon he killed the cheroot and went to bolt his door. Yawning, Brite lifted the satchel off his bed and shoved it underneath. He took a pinch of snuff and sneezed twice, had a final nightcap of whiskey. Finally the Professor kicked off his shoes and reached to turn down the lamp.

At this instant Professor Brite froze for a moment, then swung with a feline movement, drawing his revolver and cocking it. He was watching the hall door, his long head cocked. He got up and tiptoed toward it. The din from below abated a trifle. Hatfield, who had been engrossed in spying on the Professor, suddenly realized that somebody was violently shaking and kicking at the entry to the suite he was in. Now the tenant, no doubt highly indignant at being locked out of his own rooms, began shouting for the clerk and manager.

Hatfield glided to the connecting portal. "Let me in! Unlock that door, cuss it!" bellowed somebody in the hall. But the Ranger turned to an open window and looked out. The drop was not too great and he slid through, hanging from the outer sill for a moment before letting go. He landed in sandy dirt at the side of the Ace, relaxed and unhurt as he hit. Rising, he hurried away.

Brakeman Karnes and Ed Tourneau were whooping it up downstairs. A couple of young women had joined the two toughs and they were dancing. The lobby clerk appeared from the back of the hotel and put away a short ladder by which he had climbed into the locked suite and let in the rightful tenant. Sometimes drunken men overslept the stage departures, unless awakened, and the ladder came in handy when they bolted themselves in.

In the shadows down the line, Hatfield consulted with Buck. "I don't believe this Professor sidewinder will move till mornin'," said the Ranger, after giving Buck a quick sketch of what he had learned. "We need a snooze so we'll turn in and get back on watch at dawn. I'm shore Brite is the hombre who ordered the Wasp to kill Abel Pyne and the ranchers. He's just as long as a snake and drags the ground when he walks. Brite is a lot smarter than the Wasp, and he ain't here to see the sights, that's a cinch. The fact that Tourneau has so far failed to crush Evans and his pards will make Brite lash out hard. We must get into position to check him, he's mighty dangerous."

The Ranger was right about the enemy's time of departure. They had a refreshing sleep, a hearty breakfast, and waited around for a half hour before Professor Leming Brite, wearing his black coat and a purple Stetson, escorted by the Wasp and Brakeman Karnes, emerged from the Ace. Some of the Wasp's men had saddled the mustangs for the leaders, who mounted and set off north from Sherman, trailed by a score of armed toughs, riders wearing the nickel-plated insignia and white-dotted boots.

"They may be headin' for Evans' or Welder's, Buck. We'll trail at a distance and try to help our friends if need be." While the Wasp did not have his entire band along, the rest of the outlaws might be at a rendezvous outside the settlement.

The sun was hot and yellow on their right, and they were over nine miles out of Sherman as they passed the lane marked by a Box E. Lurking well to the rear on the road to the Red River, Hatfield and Buck breathed with relief as the Professor and his hands kept going, showing no sign of swinging to attack Lucius Evans.

Other horsemen were on the highway, a traveled route to the ferry across the Red. The Ranger and his youthful comrade hovered near the collection of little shacks where the ferrymen lived. A small saloon, too, was set at this point. A roomy flat-bottomed barge served as a vessel in which travelers might make a dry crossing. A strong cable was stretched across, and Negro deckhands manned long sweeps.

Several other passengers awaited transit but Hatfield did not wish to draw the attention of his quarry. At low water, as it now happened to be, riders could cross the stream although the Red was noted for its treacherous, shifting quicksands and its ability to rise many feet with little warning because of flash floods far upstream.

It was the Ranger's practice to give Buck as much instruction as possible during their forays. As they dismounted behind the crude shed serving as a bar, and watched the ferry start over with Professor Brite and the rest, Hatfield told the youth what he knew about the river.

"I've braced her before, Buck. She's mighty shifty and hard to beat. Many a pore waddy has been sucked down, tryin' to help his boss get a herd of cattle across. Cap'n

McDowell showed me a government report on her not long back. The discharge ranges from thirty-five-hundred to one-hundred-eighty thousand cubic feet per second!

"It's the southernmost of the Mississippi's big tributaries and they say twelve hundred miles long. Rises in the upper part of the Staked Plain and forms our boundary with Indian Territory. That pinkish-red color comes of suspended silt the river's carryin' off. She moves her channel whenever she has a mind to. Ever hear of the Red River rafts?"

"No, never did. What are they?" Buck was intrigued, storing away the information. Some day he hoped to know as much as his tall mentor.

"Well, the Red fetched down so many forest trees in 1828 that it jammed itself up around Shreveport, Louisiana. The dam it made was ninety miles long and the U. S. had to go to work on it. Took years to clean the channel. It pulled the same trick again durin' the War and another raft over thirty miles in length, built by the current, had to be cleared away. She's a lulu."

As the Ranger finished telling Buck about the Red, and fixed himself a quirly, the ferry reached the north bank and the passengers began leading off their saddled mounts. The

Professor, Brakeman Karnes, the Wasp and his gunslingers, collected in a band and let the others go ahead on a beaten track leading through the low bluffs and thence into the wilds of the Indian Nation. Woods could be seen beyond.

The two drank and ate at the station, resting their horses, and hung around awaiting the next crossing. The barkeeper, a one-eyed Mexican with a patch over his injured eye, joined them. He was over-friendly and too curious. The Ranger decided he might be a spy for the outlaws, tipping them off in case officers of the law arrived at the ferry. He gave Buck a wink as he assumed an open, honest mien.

"*Si,* my kid brother and I are headin' for Kansas. I got a trail herd on the way up and aim to overtake the boys and sell the cows at Dodge."

On the other side an hour later, Buck and Hatfield let two other passengers ride on. "Take the right edge, Buck, I'll watch this wing," he ordered. He had trained Buck to read sign. They were now familiar with several of the shod-hoof impressions left by the mustangs of the Professor, the Wasp and Karnes, and the bandits stayed in a bunch. Hardly a mile above the Red, Buck signaled his tall friend. The outlaws had left the road, cutting through an eroded dip in the wooded, rising land.

Hatfield crossed over and assumed the lead. There was no telling how close to the north-south way the Wasp's hideout might be. Goldy would offer certain warnings when he scented strangers.

A narrow, winding trail ran along the ridge. Now and then, through a vista of leaves seared by the hot summer sun, the Ranger could glimpse the downsweep of the valley all the way to the great river. Half a mile in, the golden sorrel sniffed and rippled his sleek hide. Immediately the officers pulled up and got down. "Hold the horses, hide off the trail, Buck. I'll go ahead on foot."

Hatfield left his heavy gear with Buck, pulling off his boots and pulling on supple moccasins in which he could walk or run much more easily. He took to the woods and flitted along, pausing now and again to listen and look. After a time he scented tobacco smoke in the warm air and soon located a trail sentinel sitting on an upended log, back to a broad tree. He bypassed the armed killer and stole on.

The Wasp's hideout was cunningly screened, nestled on a small plateau of the long, wooded ridge parallel to the river. It took the Ranger over an hour to draw close enough to make out details. There were several shacks built of forest logs, brush corrals in which the mustangs could be held. Scores of hard-eyed, heavily armed gunhands were here. He saw Professor Leming Brite, Brakeman Karnes and Ed Tourneau sitting in the shade near the largest cabin, eating and drinking.

Lying flat in thick brush out from the bandit headquarters, the Ranger observed three horsemen coming into camp. They seemed to be strangers for they were covered and questioned before being allowed to dismount, when they were led to the Wasp, who further interrogated them. Tourneau finally nodded and apparently accepted them for they mingled with the others. "Recruitin'," decided Hatfield. "Now I wonder!" He needed to get in there, ferret out the Professor's dangerous plans, and a bold idea occurred to him.

CHAPTER 5
RAIDERS

The Wasp already had a large force and the fact he was hiring more fighters pointed to a really big push. He had been checked at Evans' and the other ranches and needed further strength so he might overwhelm them. Carefully, Hatfield snaked off and later on hid himself not far from the guard down the trail. He did not have too long a wait when a rider jogged slowly in from the river road and was challenged.

"My handle is Bearpaw Smythe," announced the traveler, a squat, bearded ugly. "Jake Gordon, down in Fort Worth, told me Ed Tourneau was lookin' for good men. Well, that's me. Gordon said to ask the one-eyed Mexican at the ferry station how to find you and here I am."

"Bueno. Keep straight on and you can't miss her," the guard said. "Sing out before you barge into camp, and ask for the boss."

It was an opportunity the Ranger could

not afford to pass up. The outlaws were expecting recruits. He slid away and rejoined Buck. "I'm goin' in there and pose as a gunslingin' horsethief, Buck. I don't savvy how long I'll be and I can't leave you floatin' around loose in the brush. You better hook back to Sherman and wait for me, keep watch. I doubt if Professor Brite sticks here more than a day or two and he's liable to return to the Ace. I don't want to miss anything about him. I'll see you in town soon as possible."

Buck hated to leave but he was obedient to his tall friend's orders. Hatfield daubed some dirt on his cheeks, putting on his boots and Stetson. He had not shaved for a couple of days, and he could easily pass as a tough. He knew the manners and lingo of lawbreakers from plenty of experience with such fellows.

"I'll ride out to the main trail with you, Buck. I'll have to wait till the next ferry comes over, so it will look like I came on it. Bearpaw Smythe, who just joined up, was on the last boat."

He saw his companion off, pulling up by the north-south road through the Nations as Buck waved adios, heading for the ferry on Old Heart 7. The Ranger concealed himself, had a smoke and a pull on his canteen. After an hour, he heard and then sighted horsemen on the main trail. They had come over on the ferry which Buck would have taken back to the south shore of the Red. Half a dozen riders, strung out, passed by but there were evidently no more recruits, not this trip.

Making sure of his Colts, trying them to see how they slid in the oiled holsters, seeing that they were loaded, Hatfield swung a long leg over the golden gelding and boldly rode through the side path toward the outlaw stronghold.

Aware of where the sentry was set, he moved slowly and made plenty of noise, clearing his throat several times, letting Goldy brush dry, overhanging branches.

"Reach!" Sure enough, the bandit guard was ready beside his tree, carbine leveled.

Hatfield pulled up and stared. Then he said, "One-Eyed Juan said I'd find you around here."

"Your handle? Where you from and what you huntin'?" growled the sentinel.

"Waco Williams, they call me, and Jake Gordon told me Ed Tourneau was hirin'. I had to leave fast and goin' through Fort Worth I bumped into Gordon. Another hombre Jake sent, Bearpaw Smythe, was on the boat ahead of me. I thought I spotted a cussed marshal who's been after me, on the boat, so I didn't race for her."

"Huh! No lawmen dare poke their noses in here. You needn't worry. We've drilled more than one of the snoopin' sidewinders. They can't touch you, got no jurisdiction over the Territory." The carbine dropped. "Ride on, keep straight and you'll run right into camp. Sing out when you're there."

"Obliged." He moved along the winding track and before long came to the clearing. He drew up and called a greeting.

Armed outlaws glanced up from cards or bottles at the newcomer. "What's the trouble, Sonny?" asked a red-eyed killer impudently. Many of these fellows prided themselves on their toughness and were always trying to impress their bandit mates. Several within hearing snickered as the hulking Hatfield was addressed in such a light fashion.

Hatfield's grey-green eyes were cold and hard and after a brief exchange, the other dropped his gaze, unable to endure it. "I want to see the Boss," drawled the Ranger, with just the right inflection.

"Go over to the big shack and ask for Ed Tourneau."

He was aware of appraising looks as he dismounted and dropped rein. Mean eyes

65

glittered as they ran over the lines of the magnificent golden sorrel, for all these men were experts on horses.

Hatfield's spurs jingled as he crossed beaten ground and stopped before the open doorway of the largest hut. "Mister Tourneau here?" he called.

The Wasp was lying on a blanket-covered brush bunk. He rose and came out, gazing up into the rugged face. Hatfield stood the inspection without a flicker, aware it was a most dangerous moment. If anything happened to be sour, if by chance Tourneau recognized him from that night fight in Sherman, he could never escape.

"What is it?" asked the outlaw chief at last.

"I'm Waco Williams, suh. Happened to be passin' through Fort Worth in a powerful hurry but stopped at my amigo's, Jake Gordon's. He told me you were lookin' for fightin' men."

"I can tell from seein' you that you can shoot," nodded Tourneau. "And you seem salty though you'll have to prove it in a pinch." He had a bitter way and evil strength required to dominate the egotistical, quarrelsome gunhands who made up his band. Yet now he was not unfriendly. "What's your specialty?"

"Horseflesh, suh. I like it better than beef-steak."

"Bueno. I reckon you can tell one end of the cow from the other if need be, as well."

Hatfield had told Tourneau he was a horsethief on the dodge. Professor Leming Brite, without his coat and hat, came around the shack. Long and lanky, his wide, bony shoulders filled out his silk shirt. His over-black hair glinted with grease, inexorably fixed in place on his horse head. The man's mouth was firm, and black, shiny eyes riveted to the Ranger. Just behind Brite came Brakeman Karnes, nearly as tall as Hatfield and weighing perhaps fifty pounds more.

They stopped, appraising the tall man. The Wasp winked at Brite. "Professor, this here is Waco Williams. He's joinin' up, I reckon. Waco, any time this gent or Mister Karnes need help, you give it to 'em the same as though I told you."

"Yes, suh."

Brite nodded and pulled his silver snuff-box from his pocket. He took a pinch and sneezed. Close to, Hatfield could see the etched lines radiating from his predatory beak, the hairs of his combed sideburns. He pushed past the Wasp and entered the cabin, but Karnes remained outside.

"Yampy!" called Tourneau.

Yamping meant stealing, and Hatfield swung to see a stout outlaw come from another brush hut and approach the group by the door. "Yeah, Wasp?" Evidently the fat one's nickname corresponded with his profession. He was smooth-shaven, beads of perspiration standing out on the tight, pink flesh of his rounded face. Thin brown hair grew on his head, and his ballooned center pushed hard against his crossed cartridge belts. His weight had run over his tight half-boots.

"This is Waco Williams, Jake Gordon sent him over. Take him on." The Wasp turned and followed his master inside.

"Howdy." Yampy thrust out a plump, hairy hand, clammy with sweat. He felt the heat more than his thinner comrades. "Foller me, big feller." He waddled back the way he had come, Hatfield stalking at his heels. In Yampy's hut were stores, and from a crokersack, the fat outlaw pulled out a black cloth mask with a skeleton face painted on it. "We wear these when we're out sometimes," explained Yampy. "It not only hides you from bein' reckernized but it throws a jolt into folks. Keep it ready on you."

On wooden pegs hung a number of flat-topped Stetsons and after several tries, one was found which fitted the Ranger well enough. It had a metal insignia attached to the crown front, the shape like the usual deputy badge, but at close range the etching was only an eagle with a number under it.

"I'll daub your boots for you. Then in the dark you won't be shootin' your pards. The chief wants things this way, it's more orderly, like you're in the army."

Yampy opened a bucket of white paint, picked up a brush and daubed a circle on each of the tall officer's boots.

"Gracias, Yampy."

"Hang around and don't get into any scrapes with the other boys. If you want target practice there's a range down there in the woods, behind camp. We'll feed you and pay you accordin' to what comes in. Ask me if you need anything, don't bother the boss."

"I savvy." Hatfield nodded and Yampy waved him out, relaxing on his bunk.

The Ranger unsaddled the golden sorrel, hanging his hull on a corral fence and turning Goldy into the pen with the other mustangs. Then he returned to the outlaw circle and sat down in the shade, rolling a smoke. Some of the men were friendlier than others and before long a couple of

toughs were chatting with him on imper-
sonal matters, the price of horses and other
kindred subjects.

Presently one suggested a shooting contest
with money wagered on the result, and the
tall Hatfield was invited to join in. They
went along a footpath behind the camp and
to a range with the woods behind it. Here,
using his fine Colt, the Ranger bested them
with such ease that they were astounded
and real respect for him showed in their
eyes.

By supper time, the news of his speed and
accuracy with a revolver had spread among
the fifty outlaws. Some were convinced by
telling of the tale, others shrugged, self-
confidence undiminished. Men could be
good at target shooting but in a pinch, with
death staring them in the eye, they might
falter.

Many of the bandits preferred to sleep
outdoors. They had been given a hearty
meal of beef and hardtack. By the light of
lanterns, the interminable card games
proceeded. There was nothing to do but
gamble, drink or quarrel. Yampy sternly
checked a couple of snarling arguments
before they degenerated into shooting af-
frays.

As the camp quieted, Hatfield spread his

blanket off by himself in the shadows not far from the Wasp's lighted cabin. Brite, Karnes and Tourneau were in there. Now and then the ranger heard the clink of glass as a drink was poured. For a time he lay watching and listening. Nobody seemed to be noticing him or checking up.

Half an hour later he was crouched in the blackness on the far side of the Wasp's where he could hear through a crude window the voices of his enemies.

". . . Must double the number of men." That was the Professor.

"Plenty will be along in the next two, three days," answered the Wasp. "The word will have spread by now."

"Very well, then. In the morning the Brakeman and I will go back to Sherman. Our plans are worked out and only need to be set in motion. Actually just a few measly cowmen, Evans and his friends, are all that stand in my way. Of course we can't wait too long or the cat will be out of the bag. I flatter myself I've hidden my operations perfectly so far."

It was tantalizing to learn they had determined on a course of action yet be unable to gain an inkling of what it might be. Lucius Evans and his rancher neighbors were doomed by Brite and Wasp, that was plain, but the Ranger had already been aware of this. And before long, the three turned in, their voices thickened by too much whisky. Hatfield stole back to his bed and soon dozed off.

He ate a hearty breakfast with several outlaws who had been in the shooting contest with him, and rolled a smoke. Leming Brite, Karnes, the Wasp and a dozen armed guards, rode off toward the ferry. Hatfield and the main crew remained in camp, Yampy in command. Before noon, Ed Tourneau and his hands returned, having seen the Professor to the crossing.

During the rest of that day, and throughout the following, recruits arrived in increasing numbers, swelling the Wasp's ranks. They came from points in Texas and from the wilds of Indian Territory. What the bandits claimed was true; there was no effectual law in the Nations except what the Five Tribes cared to enforce.

Even the Federal Government could not prosecute within the confines of the savages' dominion. Killings went unpunished. Outlaw depots such as the Wasp's, handily situated to raid parties on the Kansas Trail, were safe from organized attack by Lone Star and other police forces.

Hatfield, posing as a horsethief on the dodge, had made a number of acquaintances in the hideout although most men of bandit stamp were suspicious and seldom revealed anything about their past. The Ranger was growing uneasy and restless as he waited for the enemy to move so he might diagnose the evil plans worked out by the Professor and his lieutenants. He had spent three days at the hangout and the Wasp's forces had just about doubled in number.

After breakfast the next morning, the stout Yampy, who acted as the Wasp's first sergeant, whistled them into a group so he could address them. "All right, boys. I want all the recruits up front. You others line up to the rear."

Hatfield, among the former, took his place in the ranks. When they had formed, Yampy indicated several veterans who stepped up and mixed with the newcomers.

"We're movin' out in an hour. You men in front ride with me; the others will move behind Ed Tourneau. I'll issue two days rations. Make shore your guns are in shape and you have plenty of ammo. For the new hombres just joined up, we're mighty proud of our organization and expect every feller to stand and fight when it comes to it, and obey orders. And you'll soon have a scrap, I promise you. A passel of mealy-mouthed cusses on the other side of the Red have gone for us and we aim to teach 'em a lesson. Shoot to kill any cowboy or rancher who horns in on us, savvy?

"There's three we're after special, Lucius Evans, George Welder and Dunc Kilgore, and we'll pay fifty dollars bonus to the man who downs one, ten per scalp for any of their waddies. First we're goin' to run off some of their range cattle to needle 'em, savvy? The brands you'll most likely see will be Box E, 1–2 and Slash K."

The grim, bitter Wasp lounged in the shade, smoking a thin Cuban cheroot and observing as Yampy briefed the army. Each killer wore a flat hat with the nickel insignia, and had been issued a skeleton mask. White circles had been daubed on their boots. Yampy knew how to handle such gunslingers, how to weld them into a fighting force. He was strong and more vicious than anyone else, breezily ordering them about.

Hatfield was in the crush. Mustangs saddled, ammunition issued and weapons checked, the powerful force mounted and fell into formation. Yampy was in the lead, with the recruits and a handful of trusted outlaw members acting as noncoms. Half a dozen older fellows were left to watch the hidden encampment. The Wasp, on a long-legged, yellow-hided gelding, held back with his old-timers, as Yampy moved out of the clearing.

The Ranger, perforce, went along with Yampy's crowd. But they did not take the trail to the ferry road. Instead, Yampy circled the shacks and passed the corrals and shooting range, cutting through the woods on a narrow trace. Vision cut off, Hatfield did not know whether Tourneau and his contingent were following or had gone off in another direction. He kept glancing back, trying to catch a glimpse of the Wasp, but had no luck.

CHAPTER 6
AMBUSH

For an hour they kept to the long ridge but at last Yampy swung through a slanting cut. Gravel slides let the horses down to the level of the main valley. High grass, patches of timber on rises, the huge, rotting carcasses of long-dead trees which had been uprooted and carried here by the mighty Red when it was raging, showed the effects of floodwaters, making up a wild scene. A small feeder from springs supplying the Wasp's hideout with water, zigzagged through to the river.

At last Hatfield could see to the end of the procession. The Wasp and his veterans were missing, had taken another route. Smoke drifted in the intensely blue sky from the ferry landing on the Texas side, while farther south, about where the Box E must stand, another thin column spiraled up. Leather creaked and men muttered, cursing the heat and the stinging flies and other insects.

Frankly worried as to the Wasp's aims in this double-barreled play, Hatfield now had to stick with Yampy or lose all his advantage. Two miles eastward of where the ferry crossed they pulled up at the Red. Yampy knew the river and trails, and after making sure there were no enemies in sight, the stout outlaw spoke to his followers. "You'll have to swim the channel, boys. Make sure you keep your guns and ammo dry. Foller my line, and have yore ropes ready in case a horse sinks deep, the quicksands shift a lot through here."

A curve threw tearing floods against the Texas bank, and water had cut deeply into it but the sandy bottom was now dry and covered by sun-whitened stones. The stout Yampy kicked a spur into the flank of his mustang and slid down to the stream. He splashed through the shallows, several bandits starting after him. The long file of horsemen took to the crossing and were two-thirds of the way over before it became necessary to do a little swimming.

Before long Yampy, Hatfield and the leaders were on the Texas shore, horses shaking off water, the men emptying their boots and drying themselves as far as possible. When all were safely over, Yampy began picking men for some special mission. "You — you

— you —" A fat forefinger stabbed at those he wanted. The towering Hatfield stood out and Yampy pointed at him. "You." He chose a dozen and then set the rest along the actual bank where the clay bluff was several feet high, screened by brush and low timber. He spoke in low tones for a time wih one of the Wasp's veterans, leaving this bandit in charge.

Yampy led the small group he had picked out on the range. Behind them lay the Red, their comrades hidden by the dip.

"Keep a sharp eye peeled, fellers," ordered Yampy. "We're goin' to gather us some beeves. Remember, shoot any sidewinder who comes at us. Don't get too far from me."

During the afternoon, the dozen with Yampy collected small bunches of range cattle, branded Box E, 1–2 or Slash K, and pushed them to the margin of the Red, where four riders were assigned to hold the cows from straying off again. All these men knew how to handle cattle and horses and by dark they had a herd assembled. Mounted guards were strung out for the night, and these would serve to contain the steers and also be on watch for attack.

The main bunch camped on the flat below the drop of the river bank, Hatfield among them. They ate jerked beef and hardtack washed down with water or whisky. They slept where they were, taking turns at sentry duty. At dawn Yampy routed out his picked crew and they set to work again, riding short forays south to sweep up more cows. Yampy, with a pair of field glasses, kept studying the rolling range below. He did not seem to be in any hurry. The Box E and George Welder's 1–2 were a few miles away and they had seen the smoke of breakfast fires.

At noon they ate and rested during the worst of the heat. The held steers began to complain as they browsed off the grass and what foliage was within reach. Some of the big longhorns slid down to the river to drink but were driven back by the hidden outlaws.

Late that afternoon Yampy, who seemed to be waiting for something, the field glasses to his pudgy eyes, studied a rising dust cloud to the southeast. Assisted by another rider, Hatfield had just run up a half dozen cows wearing Evans' brand. Yampy spoke to a man near him and that bandit swung, to disappear down the drop to the Red.

"This is it, boys," called Yampy, waving them in. "Here they come like the heel flies was after 'em. Set your carbines but hold fire till I give the word. Knock over as many as you can. When it gets warm and I signal, break like you're panicked and make for the river."

A score of horsemen materialized from the dust cloud. In the lead came Lucius Evans and George Welder, cowboys from both ranches with them. No doubt a range rider had noted Yampy's activity and had reported a dozen or so rustlers on hand. Evans had collected a force which would have little difficulty in driving off such a small band, rescuing the stolen cows.

"Only they don't savvy about that bunch of killers hid below the river bank," thought Hatfield.

They could now hear the war cries of the charging cowmen and the earth shook with thudding hoofs. The ranchers were moving at high speed. Yampy threw his carbine to shoulder and opened fire. Other outlaws followed suit. Hatfield had to maintain his front and threw bullets in Evans' direction but aimed high so his lead would not do any harm to his friends. To the rear, the murderous muzzles of Yampy's main crew were silently leveled, screened by brush and the killers hidden by the water-carved shoreline.

In a few minutes it would be too late to save Lucius Evans and his comrades from the deadly ambush. Many would go down, for as the excited ranchers pursued Yampy's handful to the stream; they would be close on the outlaw guns.

Hatfield was within easy reach of these enemy guns, but he was forced to act. He uttered a shrill Rebel yell, feigning to be overcome by the excitement of the battle and urged Goldy straight at the cowmen, supposedly his foes. "Let's go for the cusses, Yampy!" he bellowed, his mighty voice rising over the cracking guns.

He had reloaded his carbine and again fired it over Lucius Evans and his boys. The powerful sorrel spurted toward the oncoming riders, and Hatfield had gained twenty yards before Yampy realized he was not turning. "Come back here, you big jackass!" howled Yampy.

The outlaw game was to draw the ranchers to the river where they could be cut to pieces. The stout lieutenant was nearest to the Ranger who glanced back over a hunched shoulder, rugged jaw drawn up by a taut chinstrap. As Hatfield failed to obey orders and kept tearing on, Yampy's suspicions flared and he whipped up his rifle. The slug he sent sang within inches of the Ranger's head.

Hatfield did not like the ominous sound.

He turned in his seat and gripping with his strong knees, fired at Yampy. The killer threw up his hands and fell off his startled, dancing horse.

At this a volley roared from the brush. The concealed toughs had observed the play between Yampy and Hatfield. To the running Ranger, the lead seemed like deadly hail about him. He was aware of dirt spurts as low bullets chugged into the earth, of shrieking near-misses. Some of the outlaws were armed with heavy rifles, the big slugs droning like giant hornets. Then the officer felt metal slash his left arm just below his shoulder. The shock nearly knocked him from his saddle but he recovered, gritting his teeth as he fought the stabbing pain of torn flesh and nerves.

"Turn back, Evans!" he shouted. "Ambush! Turn, turn!"

Lucius Evans and George Welder had recognized the tall man on the golden sorrel. He signaled them off with his uninjured arm. And they had not missed that searing blast from the river bank which disclosed the presence of a strong enemy force. Lucius Evans and Welder slowed, calling orders to their waddies. Low over the sorrel, Hatfield pounded to join them as they swerved and pelted eastward below the winding line of brush marking the river. Zigzagging Goldy, Hatfield gained at every jump and the next volley from the bandits flew wild.

Looking back, he saw that Yampy had been lifted up by a couple of his aides. The stout outlaw's hat had flown off. He was not dead but wounded, gasping commands as he sagged in the arms of his friends.

The swift golden gelding soon brought the Ranger abreast of Lucius Evans.

"They were waitin' for you, Mister Evans," explained Hatfield. "I've been at their hideout across the Red, sypin' on 'em."

"You're hit!" cried Evans, seeing the blood seeping from the wounded arm. "How bad is it?"

"I can stand it. Soon as we can stop I'll tie it up. Have you seen anything of the Wasp?"

"No. Isn't he over there?" Evans was surprised.

"Tourneau and most of his old bunch broke off from us yesterday. I was afeared he might have come for you at the ranch."

Evans blinked, and looked worried, exchanging glances with Welder. "One of George's line riders along the river spotted the rustlers workin' here after noon today. Welder fetched some of his boys to my ranch and we hustled out to break it up."

Out of easy range they slowed and swung to inspect the enemy. All of Yampy's men were emerging from the brush, pulling their mustangs after them. One of them rode out and caught Yampy's horse which had trotted away but stopped to graze. The stout lieutenant was helped aboard, sagging in the saddle.

Soon night would fall over the Red River range. They were several miles from the Box E. The outlaws were mounting and setting themselves in fighting formation.

"They're comin' for us," remarked the Ranger. "We better head for your place, suh. I'm worried about where the Wasp may be."

So were Evans and Welder. Yampy's maneuvers at the river might have been not only an ambush but a draw-off.

Hatfield tore off a strip of his shirt tail and Lucius Evans helped him tie up his flesh wound. His arm felt numb, stiff with the clotted blood.

Yampy's crew, strung out with plenty of space between riders, started at them. Carbines began crackling at long range. Commanded by Ranger Hatfield the cowmen began their retreat, angling southwest for the Box E. In the open they could hold the bandits at a respectful distance even though they were outnumbered more than two to one.

The Ranger held the rear, snapping shots back at his foes, who howled at him, shook their fists and guns, spent their ammunition trying to bring him down.

CHAPTER 7
ON THE RUN

Lake Staples limped across the yard at the Box E in the lengthening shadows. He carried his pet carbine, loaded and ready for action for he had been left in charge of the ranch by his employer when Evans had hurried forth with George Welder, after some rustlers who had been operating on the Red River line.

. That morning a cinch had snapped as Staples had mounted a half-wild mustang and he had been thrown hard, injuring his right leg. For this reason and also because Lucius Evans trusted him as he might his own son, Staples had been left in charge of home base. He had two cowboys to help, beside the sixteen-year-old Wash Evans, who was sulking in his tent since his father had ordered him to stay home with the women while an interesting fight was in prospect.

Large and well-formed, Staples wore a big Stetson with curved brim, whipcord pants tucked into halfboots, a brown shirt and a dotted bandana. He had two Colts on him, spare shells for the carbine in his pockets.

Edith Evans, in a gingham dress, her chestnut hair bound by a blue ribbon, came from the kitchen and called to him. "Dinner's most ready, Lake. We've cooked up a lot and will save plenty for father and the boys when they get back."

"Bueno, Edie. I'll just take another look-see before I come inside." He adored Edith. She had brought love and gayety to him, and they intended to marry as soon as possible. Some day Staples hoped to set up a small ranch of his own.

Staples rounded the barn and could now see the stretch of rolling range toward Sherman, which lay southward of the ranch. The road from the settlement to the Red River crossing was hardly a mile west. Suddenly Staples gripped his carbine tighter and raised it. A horseman was coming lickety-split toward him.

The horse was a chunky gray mustang which could run with surprising speed for his shape and size. Staples hastily made certain there were no others in sight as he covered the rider with his finger on the trigger. The approaching man saw him but did not slacken his pace. He waved his hand several times around his Stetson, signaling he was peaceable and had important news.

As he drew close to Staples, the cowboy saw that he was a lad, lanky and clad in levis and shirt. Tow hair stuck out under the brim of his hat. Under a cocked leg rode a light rifle.

Staples relaxed a bit and watched him curiously as he pulled up, the gray dancing sideways before coming to a halt. The youth's thin face was freckled, and his nose turned up. His eyes were straight and decent.

"Howdy, mister. I reckon this is the Box E."

"S'pose it is, young feller?"

"Have you seen a tall hombre on a golden sorrel? He was here before to warn you." There was real urgency in the young voice.

That would be Jim Hatfield, thought Staples. "He ain't here now."

"I'll speak to Mister Evans, then. It's mighty important."

"He's not home either. I'm in charge," said Lake Staples.

"All right then. I'm Buck Robertson. I travel with the tall man, savvy? He left me in Sherman to watch for moves by Professor Brite and Brakeman Karnes. Well, they're on their way here right now, and they just met up with the Wasp and about fifty armed outlaws. You got twenty minutes, maybe, before they heave in sight. I cut over to warn you."

Hatfield had spoken of Buck Robertson, telling Evans that he might send his youthful comrade with a message if need be. Staples was altogether convinced and already racking his brain as to what he should do. With only a few guns he could never hold off that ravening crew in the night, they would swarm through the house and kill the scattered defenders.

Buck Robertson dismounted, breathless from his haste and the hard ride. "There ain't much time, mister."

"Come on, then, Buck. I'm Lake Staples and I work for Mister Evans. I'm your friend."

Staples turned and lurched back for the house. He had to make a difficult decision. But there was little chance that Evans and the rest could reach the Box E ahead of the Wasp and Brite, if the bandits were as close as Buck said they were.

Wash Evans came out and stared, then hurried to join the two.

"Wash! Hitch up that pair of fast blacks to the buggy, snap to it. A bunch of gunhands are comin' and we got to run your mother and sister out of here pronto."

"Shore I will, Lake." Wash's eyes livened up at the excitement.

"Buck Robertson, meet Wash Evans," called Staples, again on his way.

Two Box E waddies, Minty Johnston and Tiny Mills, sang out to him. "Saddle up, we're movin'," commanded Staples. He went into the kitchen to warn Mrs. Evans and Edith.

They did not argue long, although they still had hope that the men might get back before the Wasp struck. There was no time to pack. The women snatched bonnets and wraps and climbed into the buggy which Wash had hitched up.

"Drive the team, Wash," said Staples. "Minty, you and Tiny ride guard and hustle to Welder's. Buck and I will be along soon as we can. I'll hang near here and mebbe the boss will pull in first."

Staples cinched a hull on his horse and mounted. Jolting hurt his leg but he ignored this. With Buck on Old Heart 7, Lake Staples rode slowly eastward after the buggy and his cowboy colleagues. Dark was close at hand.

The vehicle and the two outriders kept going and dropped out of sight behind a rise topped by low brush. Here, Staples and Buck pulled up. They could see past a jut of rock, and observe the Box E in the gathering gloom.

"Here they come," said Buck, after a few minutes of tense waiting.

Staples, too, heard beating hoofs, many of them. The faint night wind brought the sounds, the low creak of leather, the jingle of metal accouterments. The riders were from westward and Lucius Evans and George Welder had gone to the Red River, on the north.

"You shore were right, Buck."

"And you were right to pull out pronto," replied Buck.

Peeking past the jut, they sighted riders wearing skeleton-face masks and flat-crowned Stetsons. More and more circled the Box E to cut off escape by victims who might be in the buildings. Gruff challenges rang out and a couple of shots crackled.

Some of the outlaws dismounted and ran toward the house. Not meeting any resistance they were soon inside and singing out the good news to their friends. In the next few minutes, night fell, the stars and a chunk of silver moon visible. Oil lamps and candles were lighted and the windows glowed yellow.

Buck and Staples could see the sinister figures moving about. "I'll creep back and try to learn what they aim to do next, Buck," whispered Lake Staples.

The cowboy flattened out and in the shadow of the rise, snaked toward the kitchen. The bandits had found the cooked food and were helping themselves to it, which somehow annoyed Staples more than anything else so far. He had been on the point of making a hearty meal and had been cheated of it by the enemy's arrival. He had to stop and hug the dirt as three men paused between him and the lighted, open rear doorway.

"We have the Box E, that's somethin', Professor," said one of them. "I reckon our trick worked. Evans was drawn off. But somehow his family and home guards have escaped."

"They may have seen us coming, Wasp. It's obvious Evans isn't home, he'd have put up a fight. Chances are the women have started for Welder's 1–2. Brakeman, we'll leave you here with fifteen men. That ought to do the job in case Evans shows up. Tourneau and I will move on the 1–2. Yampy should be along soon. Send him to Welder's with most of his recruits; we may run into resistance there."

The three leaders moved off to the ranch-house. Lake Staples had overheard enough. Not only this band but a second division under a killer named "Yampy" would strike the embattled cowmen of the Red River land. They were starting for the 1–2, and unless Welder, Evans and their main force of fighting men chanced to make for it first, which was unlikely, the attackers would find an easy objective, undermanned, with women and children in the place.

Staples withdrew, inching back to Buck. They led their horses off before mounting and riding eastward together, watching back for signs of the enemy. Lake Staples had thought it over and reached his decision. "Do you savvy where Welder's 1–2 lies, Buck?" asked the waddy.

"No, suh. I reckon I could find it, though, if yuh tell me the road."

"Keep due east by the moon for two miles and you'll shorely see their lights. There's a pond with a brook running north so if you cut the feeder you can foller it back to the buildin's in case you happen to miss out. Our folks have hardly had time to get there and instead of a half hour I figger the Wasp and his bunch are headed for Welder's to sweep 'em up.

"They can't hold as well as we could at the Box E, for their walls ain't as thick, savvy, even if they have two or three men around to add to ours. Wash and the others from here know you. Tell 'em I said to desert the 1–2 and run for it pronto. Otherwise the Wasp and this Brite sidewinder will blast 'em out, kill the men and hold the women as hostages. Those outlaws ain't got as much heart as an Indian."

Buck agreed with Staples. "You're right, Lake. The only chance you fellers have is to keep clear till Ranger Hatfield can start the ball rollin' against Professor Brite and his crew. I'll get goin'. What you aim to do?"

"I'm goin' to lie back on this trail and see if I can delay the rascals," declared Staples grimly.

Buck did not argue. Lake Staples was a brave man and meant to do his best. An hour, even half an hour gained in this dangerous game might spell the difference between victory or death. "How about the Slash K?" asked the lad. "Should our folks head there?"

"The way I see it, Brite and the Wasp, reinforced by their new bunch, can overrun Mister Kilgore's unless our main band beats 'em to it. Kilgore only hires four waddies besides his two sons. Mister Evans didn't call on the Slash K for help when he and Welder went for that small crew of rustlers on the Red, for they figured they could easy handle it, and they would have lost several hours sendin' a messenger and waitin' for what hands Mister Kilgore could spare.

"There's a chance I will contact Mister Evans and that we can stay between the enemy and our friends. It's a tossup. Otherwise the only place the women would be safe would be if they could reach Sherman. See what Kilgore and the others say. But you better ride, Buck. We've lost valuable time spielin'."

Buck Robertson nodded and swung the chunky gray mustang. Staples stayed put for a while, watching the lanky youth fade off into the moonlit plain. Then the waddy trotted his swift, strong gelding back to the brush-topped rise not far east of the Box E, where he and Buck had paused after leaving the ranch.

Staples could see lanterns flickering in the familiar yard, while lamps inside lighted the windows and open doorways of the house. Many men were outside and ready to mount their saddled animals. They were commanded by Professor Brite and the Wasp, while the outsized figure of Brakeman Karnes, who was to hold the Evans' home, showed as Brite gave his lieutenant last-minute instructions. The raiders had dropped their masks but would no doubt raise them again in action.

Lake Staples caressed his fine carbine. It was loaded and his mustang was trained so a rider might fire from the saddle without having his horse panic under him.

"I wonder where the boss is!" thought Staples. Evans must be on his way home by now, unless the chase had taken the ranchers across the Red. Sometimes bold citizens took the law into their own hands and pursued thieves and killers even into Indian Territory. Then another idea occurred to Staples and the cold sweat came out on him — suppose Yampy and his crew, mentioned by Brite, had ambushed and cut down the cowmen!

Three horsemen were fingering out from the Box E, scouts probing ahead of Professor Brite and Ed Tourneau, the Wasp, who were leading the deadly band. They came rapidly closer to Staples' hiding place and veered off from its black shadows, staring his way. The man on the right of the trio pulled rein and swung straight at Staples' brush clump, evidently aiming to check it as a matter of course.

Lake Staples shouldered his light rifle and

the crack of the weapon was sharp in the night. An unearthly howl rose from the wounded outlaw who had caught the cowboy's lead. His horse bolted past the point where Staples sat in his saddle. The other two outriders had seen the flash and hastily jerked rein, then fired at the point from which the shot had come. But their slugs whipped the bushes and harmlessly plugged into the rocky dirt, for Lake Staples had already shifted position. His next one unhorsed the nearest scout, the third spurring back to the main party and shouting warning.

At once Tourneau sent a file of gunhands to circle the brushy rise. It did not extend far and Staples knew he had to move, and fast. He had gained perhaps ten minutes here. The Wasp's men were cautious, not knowing how many antagonists might be in the bush.

Staples reloaded and kept the carbine in one hand as he slowly retreated toward Welder's 1–2. For a time he was on rolling, open plain, swept by the moonlight, few breaks in the way of low rock outcroppings and patches of blush. He pulled up and turned his horse, sat there waiting and before long riders emerged at both sides of the rise between Staples and the ranch. As they sighted him out on the plain they set up a hoarse cat-calling, challenging him. Long-range fire shrieked about him as he once more set his gelding in motion, shooting back as he ran.

For a couple of hundred yards the advance pursued him at full speed and he had to knuckle down to riding for it. When they slowed and stopped, Staples followed suit. The rest caught up and he could see the large, dark area the bunched killers covered.

Now they were sure he was alone. Half a dozen picked gunhands were detailed by the Wasp and on fast horses strung out in line they came for him. He tried to halt them with carbine lead but dared not let them get too close. The main body, led by Brite and Tourneau, kept on their course toward the 1–2 as the six killers concentrated on Staples. A couple were mounted on really superb animals, no doubt stolen by their riders. They were fresh and raced with mad speed over the rolling ground. One man was shooting a Colt, the other held his fire until he might draw nearer the target.

Staples had to ride east in order to remain between his foes and Welder's, to which he had sent Buck with the warning. Now the bandits after him allowed no breather but pounded on his trail, keeping him in sight, exchanging shots with him. The outlaw who was holding his fire streaked ahead. Shod hoofs struck sparks from rocks. Staples thought he might duel it out with the leader, drop him and make the others more respectful. He could just about stay even as it was and was being rushed when he wished to delay the party.

He slowed a trifle, then swung to shoot. He beat the killer to it, saw the flaming Colt which had not risen quite high enough as Staples let go. The waddy knew he had made a hit and then he saw one of the worst crashes he had ever observed. The big mustang seemed to take off and fly through the air like some giant monster. The rider stuck and then the horse tucked down his head and somersaulted, hitting the ground with an audible crack and rolling over and over in kicking, mad gyrations, the man's figure flung this way and that, slammed against the packed earth yet remaining attached to the heavy anchor. It was so spectacular that Staples gasped. He decided that his bullet must have pierced both man and mustang.

Cracking explosions told him the others were coming for him. The second outlaw who had been out front emptied a Colt at

Staples who pulled rein to get going once more.

Then, under him, Lake Staples felt his beautiful gelding start and quiver. He knew instantly that his mount had been wounded by a chance pistol shot, for at such range a hit by revolver was sheer luck. His position in a breath had changed from one of comparative safety to dire peril. There was no place where he might conceal himself. He was lame in a leg and could not run even if he could hope to stay ahead for a short dash.

To reach the 1–2 was now out of the question. One idea took hold of his shocked mind and he turned due south, teeth gritted. That way, and at least a half mile, lay patches of woods and some uneven country where a man might hide from hunters.

He sought to determine how badly his horse was hurt. "Where did they get you, old feller?" he muttered, caressing his pet as he sought to locate a telltale spot from which blood might be flowing.

The gelding could not tell him but had a stout heart and kept running as Staples guided. The cowboy hoped that his pursuers were not aware of the fact that his horse was injured. He was unable to find the wound but he could judge from the increasingly labored breathing that it was not a superficial one. The Colt bullet must have been fairly low, and struck where he could not reach without doing gymnastics in the saddle. There was nothing to do but push along. He could feel his gelding slowing steadily and at any moment the noble, stricken creature might fold up and crash. Lake Staples kicked loose his boot toes from the stirrups so his leg would not be caught under the heavy weight of a dying horse. He set his jaw, ready to jump and hobble on, fight his enemies to the last gasp.

CHAPTER 8
DESPERATE CAMP

Ranger Jim Hatfield, holding the rear guard for Lucius Evans and George Welder as the ranchers and their cowboys beat a slow retreat for home before Yampy's outlaw recruits, had caught the sounds of guns to the south, and Evans swung his horse and trotted to warn him.

"There's somethin' goin' on below, Ranger," said the rancher. "Doesn't sound like it's right at the ranch, though."

The tall man on the golden sorrel nodded. The strap of his Stetson was taut, bunching up his rugged chin. The gray-green eyes glinted in the silver light cast by the moon. Around his left arm was a stained, rough bandage and the shock of the wound, the long hours in the saddle and the strain of the battle, had taken their toll even upon the hickory and rawhide frame of the mighty Ranger.

A 1–2 cowboy had been left dead a mile

south of the Red River and three more waddies had been pinked in the running action. But they had given better than they had received. Eight to ten bandits, including Yampy, had either been knocked out of their saddles or slashed so badly that they had fallen out of the procession. Respect for Hatfield's Colts, for the guns of the hardbitten cowmen, had held off the wolfish pack, prevented Yampy's crew from pressing too near those dangerous muzzles.

They had paused for water at a brook, men holding back the outlaws while their comrades drank or bound their hurts. Dark had come and Yampy's gunhands had spread out in a line designed to sweep them along. Dust rolled in thick, slowly settling billows and many of Evans' friends had raised bandannas to strain it from the air they sucked in, while the gunhands wore their skeleton masks.

Now and then the stubbornly retreating waddies would glimpse a dark centaur figure after them while flaming pistols and carbines stabbed back and forth with snarling fury. Shouts and cursing threats, the creak of leather, whinnying of excited mustangs joined the echoing explosions of guns.

In brief gaps, the running victims of

Professor Leming Brite's evil designs had heard shooting to the south of them. Hatfield sought to diagnose what it meant. "It could be the Wasp. And we don't savvy just where Brite is. He could have left Sherman and hooked up with Tourneau and his crew."

They could now see the lights in the Box E ranchhouse. Yampy's recruits were not pushing them too fast. It reminded Hatfield of the way steers might be driven when the herders wished to direct them into a corral without stampeding them.

The men were tired and looking forward to the sanctuary of the Box E, left in charge of Lake Staples. They needed rest, food and drink. Lathered mounts must have a breather. And there was tension in such a running scrap for the next breath might bring leaden death.

"I'll go ahead and check up at your home, Mister Evans," said Hatfield. "We better not rush in too blind."

Lucius Evans took the officer's place as commander of the rear guard while the Ranger spoke softly to Goldy, picking up his pace. He galloped past the strung-out cowboys and made for the Box E. They were quiet and peaceful in the moonlight, the barn and bunkhouse darkly shadowed, the windows and open doors of the house itself yellow with the subdued glow of oil lamps.

The man on the golden sorrel circled to a point where he could command a view of the main yard. Nobody seemed to be stirring. Staples might be lying low, hearing the noises of the approaching battle. "I don't like the smell of it," muttered the tall man and Goldy tossed his head, rippling his hide as though to agree.

He had moved in a bit closer as he strove to make certain about the Box E. An oversized man wearing a flat-crowned Stetson stepped back from an open side entry, the light catching the gunmetal glint of double barrels, a sawed-off shotgun in his hand. Disappointment flooded the Ranger. "Brakeman Karnes!" he growled. He sighted another head as a killer bobbed up and peeked out a window. There was no doubt about it now. Though he had not spied Professor Brite or the Wasp, Hatfield was aware that the enemy held the ranch.

It was bad news that he must carry back to the exhausted men. They were almost within rifle shot and he swung his horse and lined out to rejoin Evans and Welder. The gunslingers inside must have had him in sight, as they lurked behind the walls to cut down the returning band, for they opened up on him as he streaked off, the slugs singing about him as he ran.

He sang out in stentorian tones to warn his friends as he neared them. Soon he was at Lucius Evans' side, the stoutish Welder close at hand. "Brite has the Box E, gents," reported the Ranger.

It was shocking to Evans, for though two of his sons, Mike and Jeff, were riding with their father, Mrs. Evans and Edith, Wash, Lake Staples and two trusted hands had been left at the home station. For a moment Evans was unable to speak. Then, his voice choked, he asked, "No sign of anything?"

Welder was swearing, teeth gritted. Hatfield knew what Evans wished to know. "No sign, suh, I'm sorry to say. I spied Brakeman Karnes in the house. They're set and waitin' to slash us to pieces when we ride home."

"Make for my place, it ain't far," growled George Welder. "I'm mighty sorry, Lucius. Mebbe they're bein' held prisoner and we can rescue 'em later."

The Box E boss sagged in his saddle. The unhappy tidings spread like wildfire through the party and gloom took the place of freshened hope they had had with arrival at the ranch.

"All right, boys," said the Ranger, voice

strong and steady. "We're goin' over to the 1–2. Mebbe we'll find our friends there waitin' for us. Hold 'em off, now, and we'll make it." He was a tower of strength. The cowboys would follow such a man, obey him without question. Lucius Evans, comforted by his friend Welder, braced himself.

They swung eastward. Howls came from outlaw throats at this. A line of pelting, skeleton-masked killers, disappointed too because the victims had not stepped into the trap, swirled down seeking to cut them off and drive them back on the Box E. The gun voices stepped up as the Ranger and his crew beat them off.

The pursuers made contact with Karnes at the Box E. Then they continued the run.

Hatfield had had time to think it over. If the Wasp and Brite had seized the Box E, they could have gone on and taken the 1–2 with little effort. "I s'pose they left the Brakeman and some sharpshooters to ambush us," he decided.

He consulted again with Evans and Welder. "We'll see how your home is fixed, Mister Welder. But these horses will tucker out before long and our boys are hardpressed. Is there any stretch of rough country where we can hole up before daylight? Chances are this bunch after us will be reinforced by Brite and the Wasp's main crew."

"There's what's called the brakes, not far south of us," answered Welder.

The moon was an hour older as they neared the 1–2. As it had been at the Box E, lights glowed in the ranchhouse and all was apparently peaceful. Longing eyes fixed on the haven. Once more the scouting Ranger, traveling on his last reserves of strength, made a lone foray to check up. And a second time he sighted the flat-topped Stetsons with glinting nickel badges, men waiting in there for them.

Returning to Evans and Welder, he took command again. "They're here too, gents. I'll lay a thousand to a doughnut the Professor and Tourneau already hold Kilgore's Slash K. We can't take a chance and make the run to Kilgore's; we'll ride straight for the brakes. How about a volunteer to head for Slash K, just in case the outlaws ain't been there yet? Anybody feel fresh enough?"

"I'll go," said Mike Evans.

"Bueno. Don't let 'em down you. See who's there and fetch us word at the brakes."

"We'll camp at Cool Spring, son," said Lucius Evans.

They slowed and held the enemy until Mike Evans had galloped off, rounding the 1–2 and heading for Kilgore's. Then they swung south and, fighting all the way, finally sighted the dark, rising section where the rolling plains were broken by great rock outcroppings and stands of virgin timber. Into the blackness went the weary riders, and with their mounts safely in the background, took cover from which they could blast off the bandit wolves.

There were not so many of the latter after the hard struggle. Some had sneaked away in the crush, others had been shot out of the picture. None would venture against the sharpshooting Ranger and his friends as they lay safely behind rocks and the thick boles of giant spruce. They drew up, howling and wasting lead for a time. But they were tired and hungry as well as the cowmen. Soon they turned and rode away toward the Box E.

With deep relief the cowboys saw them go. They could drink from warm canteens, bind their hurts, chew on hardtack and strips of dried beef which some had brought in their saddle pockets and now shared with comrades. Quirlies were rolled and men gratefully inhaled the smoke.

Hatfield sat down by Evans after tearing off another strip of his shirt tail. He moistened it with water and rebandaged his stiffened arm. His throat felt dry as flannel and the sips of stale, lukewarm water did little to alleviate the burning thirst he suffered.

"How far is Cool Spring, suh?" he asked the rancher, who sat hunched over, arms folded.

"Three quarters of a mile, south and a bit east," replied Lucius Evans. He had tight hold of himself but his voice was grim. "Rough goin'."

"We better spare an hour here, then. After that we'll make for it. Maybe Jeff or one of the younger boys will scout over ahead of us in case Mike should show up before we get there."

A cowboy volunteered for sentry duty and the others lay down where they were, the Ranger among them, and soon were asleep.

It seemed no time at all before they were roused. Again they resumed the retreat, for Hatfield did not wish to remain too close to the point where the outlaws had last seen them. The Wasp and the main bunch might be along and the small party with the

Ranger was in no condition for another hard fight against fresh foes.

Jeff Evans had gone on ahead to Cool Spring. Though the rest had been brief it had made it possible for them to continue.

Harve Loman, a Box E waddy who knew every inch of the brakes, from chasing cows through it, acted as guide, his friends strung out behind him. Evans and others, too, were well acquainted with this terrain. At times they could ride a few hundred yards but often had to dismount and lead their horses after them to pass rougher areas. The smell of conifers was sharply distinct in the cool darkness as they worked slowly along.

The Ranger held on with Indian fortitude, enduring from step to step and shutting off the future, hoping only that Cool Spring lived up to its name. The minutes dragged endlessly, his wound hurt and the need for sleep weighted his eyelids. But he permitted no sign of faltering to show.

"We're most there," croaked Lucius Evans at long last.

A low warning hissed back along the ragged column. They stopped and kept silent and soon heard the slow approach of someone coming through the brakes. There was a challenge, a quick reply.

It was Jeff Evans. "Dad! I got there all

right. Mike isn't in yet. But I stumbled over Handsome, Lake's pet gelding, lyin' dead a few paces from the springs!"

"No sign of Staples himself?" asked Hatfield.

"Nope. His saddle's gone, though."

"Did it look like there were any others with Lake, son?" inquired Evans.

"No suh. I cast around but I couldn't pick up any sign save Lake's," answered Jeff.

"Lake would never have left 'em unless it was all over or he just couldn't help it," growled Lucius Evans.

This was another blow to what sparse comfort remained to Evans and Welder. Up to now there had been the possibility that Staples might somehow have managed to rescue the women, lead the survivors to safety.

Silently they resumed the march and soon came to the deep springs bubbling from the split rocks. Hatfield flattened out, sucking in long draughts of cold, delicious water. A sentinel was posted and the worn party slept.

CHAPTER 9
MESSAGE

The woods were chilly in the gray of the new dawn filtering through the trees. Jim Hatfield started awake as the camp sentry crossed the small clearing and bent over Lucius Evans, shaking the rancher chief awake. Hatfield stood up, his muscles stiff from lying in a cramped position. He could scarcely raise his left arm; it had swollen and above the elbow the flesh burned, deeply inflamed. It needed skillful and careful attention while he needed a hot meal and time off, although the few hours' rest made it possible for him to keep going.

The officer heard the sentinel's report to Evans. "There's a lone hombre comin' up the line, suh. He's movin' mighty slow and careful and huggin' the line of the woods."

Mike Evans had come in during the night. Lucius had heard his eldest son's report on the Slash K, that Kilgore was not there and that the spread was held by enemy raiders, a detail of the Wasp's gunhands. Welder and Evans rose, unkinking their knees and elbows, grunting, and drank from the pools. The Ranger joined the men, and tried to tidy himself up. Whiskers stood out wirily on his rugged face, his clothing was stained and ripped from the long riding and fighting he had undergone.

There wasn't much to eat, a mouthful or two apiece left in the saddle pockets. The horses had been picketed and waddies led them to water at the lower springs. Goldy came trotting to Hatfield at the tall man's whistle. He saddled the golden sorrel and went with several more to check up on the rider reported by Olie Olsen, a Box E retainer.

At the rim of the trees, which grew to the edge of rolling plains characterizing the land, the Ranger focused his field glasses on the horseman. The fellow from the south would emerge from the shelter of the woods, move cautiously along for fifty yards, then duck back for a time. He seemed fearful of staying out in the clear. He slumped in his seat and his hat was small, unlike a cowboy's wide Stetson. Furtively, showing himself for a minute or two, he worked north.

"That's a mule he's on," remarked the Ranger to Lucius Evans.

The rancher nodded, his eyes red and white lines around his lips. Older than the others, shocked by dread of his loved ones' fate, Evans had not been able to sleep much and did not have the resiliency of the powerful young fellows who rode for him.

The rider came a bit closer, and once more hid himself. As he emerged, Hatfield gave a surprised exclamation. The light was better and he had had a good look at the face and figure as the approaching fugitive straightened up and glanced their way. "Mister Evans, take a peek! I believe it's Lake Staples."

Evans jumped up and seized the glasses which Hatfield held out to him. He watched for a time and then swung to bring out his horse. "It shore is, Ranger! Come on, we'll meet him."

Staples, when he saw them coming, broke and made for the brush. But soon he realized who it was and came out, waving and calling to them. The Ranger and Evans were first at his side and Hatfield let the agonized rancher have his say.

Evans gripped Staples' hand. The cowboy's face was worn with anxiety, and he had on a soft hat with a narrow brim, pulled down on his goodlooking head. He had his carbine and Colts and was not hurt save for scratches and a few bruises.

"Yes suh. Yes suh," he gasped, happy to see his friends. "We seen the cusses comin' and before that, Buck Robertson pulled in at the ranch with a warnin'." He nodded to the Ranger. "Your young pard, suh. He's a lad to ride the river with if I ever saw one."

"What about the folks?" Evans and Welder, who had come up, pressed Staples for the vital news.

"I done started Mrs. Evans, Edith, Wash and the two boys off to Mister Welder's. Buck and I lay back to see what held. We'd hardly pulled out when that Professor vermin and the Wasp pulled in. They left Brakeman Karnes and a crew to hold the ranch and headed straight for the 1–2. It was plain they could take Mister Welder's without much of a scrap, so I hustled Buck with a warnin' for the folks to vacate pronto.

"I lay back and tried to delay Brite and Tourneau. I stung 'em a bit, then Handsome was hit in the vitals, I had to make for the nearest woods and didn't figure I'd get there. But Handsome made it, he was the best horse a man ever had." Staples was sad at loss of his equine friend.

"What did Buck aim to do next, go on to Mister Kilgore's?" inquired Hatfield. "Our friends aren't there, and the enemy holds the Slash K house just like they do the others."

"Then they must have made for Sherman, with Mister Kilgore and Buck to lead 'em," declared Lake Staples.

"That's it," cried George Welder, with relief in his voice. "I'll bet they made it safe in the dark, Lucius."

It was a real straw at which to clutch and the natural optimism of the pioneer Red River ranchers came to the fore. Evans and Welder both cheered up, and the cowboys relaxed. Hatfield spoke with Staples for a time.

"I got the hat from some engineers I met down the line," explained Staples. "My Stetson flew off in the dark and I didn't have time to hunt for it, they were after me too close for comfort. I made the brakes finally a few jumps ahead and got to Cool Spring. Then poor Handsome dropped dead. I believe he kept goin' on his nerve to take me out of that jam."

The Ranger questioned the cowboy. Staples had met a small party of engineers whose campfire he had sighted as he trudged on south along the fringe of the brakes, not daring to venture, unmounted, between the Box E and rough country because the enemy might be hunting for him and run him down. The engineers had fed him, loaned him a mule and a felt hat, and he had decided to chance it and try to slip through to Sherman on the north route which he believed Buck and Kilgore would have followed under cover of night had they made for town. The mute had proved a disappointment since he would trot only when he happened to be in the mood. Spurring just made him more stubborn.

"I had to beg him like a Dutch uncle before he would pick up his hoofs," complained Staples. "I'm still mighty lame or I'd have took to the Snake Track."

"What's that?" asked the Ranger.

"It's a windin', narrow way through to the west side of the brakes," explained Lucius Evans.

"We better paddle for it, gents," drawled the Ranger. "Sherman's the answer. The three ranches are goners, Brite and the Wasp hold 'em and we'd be cleaned out if we attack with so few hands and worn to a frazzle as we are. Besides, most of our ammunition has been shot away. We'll run for the settlement and catch our wind. By now, Kilgore and your folks must have arrived there." His voice was calm and sure, with no hint in it of what he was undergoing. But the tall officer knew he must have relief before he regained his prime fighting power to brace Leming Brite.

The leaders were against showing themselves on open range between the brakes and the Red River, with the swarming outlaws on the prod. They were in no condition to conduct another extended, running battle. With Mike Evans as guide, they shoved into the woods and began the slow, tortuous march across the wild brakes.

As they sighted Sherman in the late afternoon, a stage was pulling into town from the southeast. Big wagons were slowly rolling in to the busy junction.

"There's Dunc Kilgore and some of our pards," called Jeff Evans.

Buck Robertson was with the Slash K chief and several waddies of the three spreads, men who had been home guards. It was a joyful meeting. The wiry, dour Kilgore, usually with little to say for himself, greeted them volubly, his thin, bearded face wreathed in a wide grin. He shook hands with his friends and news was quickly exchanged. The women and children were safe at the homes of friends in Sherman.

After a breather to rest the horses and men on their arrival in town, Kilgore had swung out to see if he could find Evans' party. They had been on the go all day and had found the home range patrolled by outlaws. Several times they had been fired on and forced to retreat. Dusty and worn, they had finally turned back to the settlement.

Soon the men were reunited with their families. Lake Staples had found his Edith once more. The Ranger, Buck at his side, checked around the center but there seemed to be no sign of Brite and the Wasp. The officer was uneasy but sat down for a hot meal and drink. He kept watching through the restaurant window for his foes. "You got the steam to spy out the Ace, in case Brite may have come in, Buck?" he asked.

"Shore. I had a nap, and I'm fine."

Goldy and Old Heart 7 had been attended to before they had thought of themselves. The Ranger went into a store to buy ointment and clean bandages while Buck trotted to the hotel where Brite had his room.

Soon the youth was back, joining the tall officer in the square. "The clerk says the Professor's out for a few days. There's a new padlock on Brite's door. I think I could pry the nails out of the hasp if I wasn't caught workin'. They ain't in deep."

"Bueno. I need sleep but I reckon I need a peek at Brite's papers a heap more. Help me bind this up." Hatfield had a hunch as

120

to the Professor's intentions, from information Lake Staples had come upon. He wished to verify this.

Plenty of good food and steaming coffee had helped. But his arm was paining, badly swollen. He borrowed a small chisel and a hammer from the wrangler at the livery stable where they had left their horses. Buck tucked the tools inside his shirt and Hatfield trailed him over to the Ace. The tall man leaned against the wall at the turn down the gallery as Buck went to work. He gave warning when a couple of guests passed through. Buck quit until they had gone by. Soon the youth had pried the nails from the wood and the Professor's door could be opened.

Hatfield went inside and shut the portal, Buck loosely replacing the lock and standing watch. Under the Professor's bed he found the suitcase and in the bag were Brite's papers. The officer studied them for a time, put them back and looked over what Brakeman Karnes had in his satchel.

When he was finished, they did a skillful job of repairing the lock. Dirt was rubbed into cracks where splinters could not be stuck back. "That ought to do it," said the Ranger. "If they do notice it, they'll figger it was thieves huntin' loot, I figger."

His head felt light and he had difficulty in keeping straight as he walked across the plaza, crowded with people. The wound was infected and he might have fever, he decided. A stage, wheels screeching as the driver made a sharp turn into the square, plying his long whip as he whooped it up and urged his horses to a gallop, came to a halt up at the station. Such gentry always liked to make a theatrical finish and never thought of walking their steeds into town if it could be helped.

Passengers were getting down. "Jim! There's Sis!" cried Buck.

Ill as he was, the sight of Anita Robertson was a sudden, tremendous comfort to the officer. They crossed to greet her, and Buck took her bag after he had kissed her.

"Anita, you're a sight for sore eyes!" declared the Ranger.

She smiled up at him. "I've brought you a message from Captain Bill, Jim. He thought it so important that he asked me to hurry here."

Anita handed him a letter from McDowell.

Spots swam before his gray-green eyes as he read the Ranger captain's bold scrawl.

"This adds up to what I've figured, Anita,"

he nodded.

He reeled and she clutched his hand, her smile disappearing.

"Jim, you're ill! Why, you're burning with fever."

"He's got a nasty puncture in his left arm, Sis," said Buck.

Now she inspected the bandaged left arm, the swollen flesh a deep red below the wrappings. "It's infected. You'll have to get to bed and let me poultice your wound."

"Yes, ma'am," agreed the tall man, meekly enough.

He had kept the room rented at a small hotel across the way, and retired to it. Anita bustled about, visiting the kitchen for hot water and meal, sending Buck for some medical preparation she needed. Soon she had clapped on the steaming poultice, and the weary Ranger closed his eyes.

CHAPTER 10
MUSHROOM TOWN

When Hatfield awoke he had trouble in remembering just where he was and why. He felt washed out and Anita Robertson sat at his side. Sunlight streamed in under the curtain she had fixed over the upper part of the window.

"I reckon I slept right through," he murmured.

"Jim! Are you feeling better?" she asked anxiously.

"Yes, I can get up."

"No, you mustn't. Here, take a drink of water. You were out of your head for a while."

The cool drink was good. "How long I been here?"

"Two days and nights, Jim. Your wound is much better."

"Where's Buck?"

"He's gone out, but he's slept by you every night to tend to you. Mister Evans and your other friends have been here inquiring after you, while Edith and her mother have helped me nurse you."

"Has Evans tried to muster help in town?"

"Yes, but he hasn't had much luck. You know the former marshal was killed by the toughs and so far nobody will take his job. Folks fear the Wasp. The cowmen have tried to take back their homes but they were beaten off. Buck says that awful Professor Brite rode into town late at night with some armed outlaws and picked up his baggage at the Ace. He checked out of the hotel."

"Huh! I better get goin'. It's lucky Brite didn't savvy just where Evans, Welder and Kilgore are hidin'. He'd have gone for 'em. He may attack 'em yet for he needs to be shut of 'em."

She begged him to stay where he was, at least until the next day, and finally he agreed for he knew he could not yet operate with full efficiency. After dark fell Anita lighted the lamp and then brought supper on a tray. They ate together, and soon Buck Robertson came along, delighted to find his mentor improved.

"Jim, I got real news! A big mushroom town has sprung up about four miles south of the Red River, right close to the Box E buildin's. They've brought shacks on rollers and wheels, loads of logs and lumber, tents and hide shelters. That settlement went up like magic and is still at it, growin' every hour. People are crowdin' in like they'd gone loco, buyin' lots and parcels. They come in wagons and buggies, even walkin'. They've named her Denison and already you'll have a fight on your hands if you say anything but good about the place. It's the all-firedest boom I ever heard of."

Hatfield nodded. "So it's out in the open. Professor Brite's makin' money. I'll go for the rascal in the mornin'."

Buck's tidings hardly came as a surprise to the officer for through his investigation of the Professor's papers and McDowell's warning message carried by Anita, he had deduced why Leming Brite had been in such a hurry to drive off the ranchers and seize their lands. The cat was out of the bag so far as the public was concerned. The Ranger's moves had delayed Professor Brite, prevented him from forever silencing Evans, Welder and Kilgore, who were still dangerous to his plans. But Brite held possession and was in control.

Another long sleep did wonders for Hatfield. Next morning he rose and washed, put on a new shirt Buck had bought for him in town. The wound no longer ached.

Anita's treatment had started the healing and the Ranger could use his arm well enough, a neat bandage under his sleeve.

After a hearty breakfast and a smoke he took his leave of Anita. At the livery stable corral the golden gelding trotted over to greet him, and the horse had also profited by the rest.

Buck joined him. They rode up the square and swung off on a side street. The lad guided the Ranger to a home in town where Lucius Evans and his family were being boarded by friends. The Welders and the Kilgores were close at hand, their men camped in the barns and sheds.

Evans was glad to see the tall man again ready for action. "It looks bad, Ranger. Brite holds our ranches. I guess they've told you of that mushroom settlement in my back yard."

"Yes suh. That's why Brite was so all-fired anxious to shove you away. I hope your title and those of your pards are free, clear and recorded proper-like in Austin."

"We got our deeds," nodded Evans. "And we took care of everything accordin' to law."

"Bueno. Then that's in your favor even if Professor Brite does hold the properties. He's sellin' them off, from what Buck tells me. You could win finally in court but that would take months and by then the Professor will have made his pile and sashayed. He'll hire lawyers and I know that he's forged warranties and notes givin' him title to your range for I saw 'em among his papers. I'm goin' out now and take a peek at Denison."

"You want us along?" inquired Lucius Evans.

The Ranger shook his head. "Not this trip. I better scout first. They'll be watchin' for us, no doubt. And you must take care of yourselves, Mister Evans. Brite's position would be far stronger if he was shut of you. Stick close together here in Sherman, savvy? Buy plenty of ammunition and keep a guard out. You can fight off an army if you're in the right kind of shelter."

"All right. I'll wait till I hear from you. I got a few pards in town who are willin' to help us out in a pinch."

"Fine. Collect as many as you are able. We'll need 'em, and more too."

Buck and Hatfield took their leave of the rancher chief, and rode north out of Sherman. Since dawn, newcomers en route to the boom town of Denison had been parading on the road, hustling to the place, hoping to get there early before all the opportunities to get rich quick had evaporated.

Horsemen, wagons and buggies were in the procession, and the dust never had time to settle, stirred by hundreds of hoofs.

They bypassed slow-moving oxen, drawing one-room structures mounted on low carriers equipped with rollers or small wheels. And as they neared the Box E, which lay only a short distance from the infant settlement, they could see other processions from various points of the compass converging on Denison. Smoke from cook fires hung in the intensely blue sky. Snatches of excited talk floated to the Ranger's and Buck's ears as they swung out to ride by slower travelers or parties catching a brief rest.

"Sherman's got nothin' on us," boasted a large, middle-aged boomer, his eyes gleaming with excitement. He had not yet even reached his goal but he was primed with rumors. "There's already more saloons and General Sheridan's goin' to build an Army supply depot right in the center."

"I hear our new county will spread across the Red and take in a lot of Indian Territory soon," said another.

"Yessuh," cried a third. "We'll have the biggest city this side of New York. Wait and see."

Others were talking of stage lines, railroads, shops, of the sudden fortunes men were making overnight in Denison simply by buying a bit of land and reselling the next day at several times the price paid.

"What did I tell you, Jim?" said Buck. "Folks have gone loco."

But Hatfield had seen similar rushes elsewhere. He knew the intense fever which seized on humanity at such moments. It was like a gold rush, and land speculation in Texas was at its height. The steel rails were rapidly pushing out in all directions after the War and with them ran the booms.

As they drew in on Denison the scene grew wilder, men and women rushing this way and that. Streets had been hastily marked out by driving stakes and putting up crude signs on poles. "Main Street" was the center of it all. Watching for enemies, Hatfield and Buck joined the crush. Auctioneers were busy selling plots of land, while individuals were making deals, one disposing of a parcel as soon as he had bought, sometimes at four or five times the price.

Portable cabins had been unloaded haphazardly, tents hastily erected. A barrel of whisky on two chunks of wood, a few tin mugs and a tarpaulin cover set up a man as a saloonkeeper, and all were doing a rushing trade. A pair of dice and packs of cards, a crude table shaded from the sun likewise served as a gambling parlor for the parasites who had been among the first to arrive.

Even dancehalls had been started with dancehall women who had been hurried in by carriage. Rude music helped swell the babel rising to the warm Texas sky. Lucky operators who had already made a killing by transfer of property were celebrating their good fortune and whooping it up. Hammers banged as owners and carpenters hired at triple wages constructed more permanent buildings from loads of lumber brought from distant forests. All these were in demand before they were completed. The energy of the populace was astounding.

So far, Hatfield and Buck, crowded this way and that by bustling, hurrying folks, blind to everything save their own affairs, had seen nothing of their enemies. The Wasp and his crew would be more or less lost in the shuffle, and many must be still at the three ranches, holding them down so the rightful owners could not reclaim them.

"There'll be fifty thousand people here inside a month!" gasped a passerby to a friend as they trotted by, gripping land deeds in their hands.

"Land will jump a hundred times over," replied the other.

There were plenty of rough characters around, though none looked familiar to the officer and his companion. Armed and bearded, off the plains or over from the Territory, pouring into Denison from every angle, they seized their chance to prey on the honest dealers and settlers who had come to town.

"I s'pose Brite can hire as many gunhands as he needs, from among these hombres," observed the Ranger. "Let's go on to the next corner, Buck."

It was slow pushing through the teeming crowds. Cursing teamsters, plying the whip, tried to get their loads in and out, but were blocked by sheer masses of humanity. At the intersection, they saw a plaza marked by crude posts driven into the ground. In a prize location stood a log shack which had undoubtedly been rolled there. Beside it, a commodius structure was almost finished. A sign as large as the front of the shack rose over the flat roof.

"BRITE DEVELOPMENT CO.
LOTS & PARCELS FOR SALE"

The door stood open, and a wide, glassless window, a counter behind it, served as the Professor's business quarters until the larger edifice should be ready for occupancy. Abreast of the window, Hatfield saw Brite inside behind the counter, with aides and secretaries busily making out deeds and other documents. Buyers crowded around. The Professor wore a frock coat and high silk hat, and he was making sale after sale as eager people thrust money into his hands.

"There's the Wasp, Buck," warned Hatfield. "We better shift."

Ed Tourneau had emerged from a nearby tent saloon, wiping his mouth with the back of his sleeve. He slouched against a corner of Brite's, out of the crush, his evil eyes catching the light as he looked over the crowd. Suddenly his gaze settled on Hatfield, who was unobtrusively retreating.

He acted as though stuck by a sharp pin, violently jumping. His hand dropped to a holstered Colt but he did not draw and fire. The Ranger was ready for a duel if it came to that, but perhaps the killers had been issued orders not to create unnecessary panics that would be bad for business. Tourneau swung, and called to some of his followers who were in the tent drinking. They hurried out and went to pick up their horses, waiting behind the buildings.

Hatfield and Buck were in the clear as the Wasp and a dozen of his gunhands burst out of Denison and came at them, guns rising. The golden sorrel and Old Heart 7 picked up their heels, the Wasp in full cry after them. The Ranger headed toward the brakes that rose in the southeast. With the bustling Denison left behind, the Wasp opened fire.

The officer replied with his Colt, and Buck unshipped his light rifle. The speed of their horses kept them out in front. Here and there were parties making for Denison, and these stared at the running fight over the rolling plains.

CHAPTER 11
GUN PRESSURE

The Wasp kept after them for about a mile, hoping that some accident might befall Goldy or Old Heart 7, that a lucky shot might strike so that the fugitives could be run down and slain. But as he was drawn farther and farther off base, perhaps suspecting an ambush and finding the retreating pair on superior mounts, Ed Tourneau pulled up. Bursts of slugs and profanity followed the Ranger.

Hatfield and Buck had had a peek at Denison, and now they set their course back to Sherman, passing south of the Box E. Enemy eyes observed them from the ranchhouse and a couple of long tries from heavy rifles kicked up dirt short of them.

"Brite is shore entrenched," remarked Hatfield. "It's goin' to be a job routin' out the sidewinder, Buck."

He was weighing the situation, figuring how to defeat the power of the foe.

Back in Sherman that afternoon, the Ranger consulted with Lucius Evans, George Welder and Duncan Kilgore at Avery's, the square house where the Box E boss and his family had found haven. Avery was sixty, and silver-haired, his wife about the same age. Their children had grown up and left home, and the elderly couple had taken in their friends off the neighboring range.

"We can't wait much longer, gents," declared the Ranger. "Brite can only be stopped by force. He's makin' big money out there at the new town site. How many fightin' men you been able to collect in Sherman?"

They had perhaps a dozen to add to their own forces. It was not too large a band to pit against the gathering strength of Leming Brite and the Wasp. "I've got an idea workin' out, though," said Hatfield. "Have your men keep their guns handy and in prime condition, suh. They better stick within easy call, too. I wouldn't be at all s'prised if Brite takes another swipe at you. His forged deeds will go over a lot easier if the s'posed sellers such as yourself are not alive to talk."

When he had finished giving instructions to the rancher chiefs he visited a hardware store, Buck in tow. Here he brought black

136

and red paints, brushes and heavy white sheets of paper. Retiring to the hotel room and assisted by Anita, they manufactured a number of signs and notices on large squares of the paper and hung them around the walls to dry.

As dark fell over the bustling junction they finished the task. The three ate together at a nearby restaurant. "Buck and I better have a snooze while we can," said the Ranger. "It will be mighty late before we can nose into Denison again."

The two turned in at their hotel room and slept for a couple of hours. Then the Ranger roused, alert as he opened his eyes. Staccato gunfire and confused yells echoed in Sherman, rising over the usual music and general wassail. Hatfield and Buck pulled on their boots, and strapped on hats and cartridge belts. The door latch rattled and Lake Staples' excited voice sang out to them.

"Ranger! The Skeleton Riders are in town, masses of 'em, attackin' Avery's."

Buck pulled the bolt and Staples stood there, eyes flashing with excitement. "I better hurry back," said the waddy. "They'll need every hand. Mister Evans sent me to warn you."

Staples ran down the rickety stairs and

outside, Hatfield and Buck trailing him. Curious crowds surged westward from the square, hunting safe positions from which to observe the sudden attack. The Ranger paused at a turn, where a building corner jutted. He could look down the lamp lighted street, with homes and small stores on either side, and see the horsemen in skeleton masks and the flat-topped hats with the nickel insignia. Brite had sent the Wasp with his horde of veterans and killers newly hired in the Territory and Denison, to deal with Lucius Evans and his friends.

Carbines, shotguns and Colts blared at close range as the riders poured metal into Avery's, but they kept moving, for replies snarled from the windows and the passages between the house and its neighbors were swept by sharpshooters in the stable and a tool shed. A writhing mustang, screaming and kicking its legs, lay on its back in the dust, its owner unmoving where he had landed. The heavy reports roared in the street, which had cleared of all neutrals as the conflict opened.

Lake Staples dropped to a knee, and threw up his carbine, snugging it to his burly shoulder. He took aim and another of the Wasp's killers jumped, sagged in his saddle and then rode out of the melee as Staples let go. Hatfield and Buck worked their accurate light rifles, with plenty of targets. They could hear Tourneau shouting at his fighters, "Get in there! Rush 'em, up on the porch."

A surge of gunhands roared to the low veranda and many jumped down to charge the door at Avery's. Angled weapons spat them from two front windows. "Come on, come on," cried Hatfield, running down the wooden sidewalk. Buck and Staples were right with him and they knelt across the road from the besieged house, pouring lead into the massed outlaws. They worked their guns as fast as they could, shrieking metal slashing the bolder bandits who had made the Avery's porch.

Masked attackers were dropping, staggering, shrieking as they felt the sharp counter. The Wasp kept moving, yelling to his men. He noted the trouble across the way and swung a detail at Hatfield and his two aides. Blasts from Colts and spreading buckshot drove the trio back off the sidewalk and they ran through a dark path beside a single-storied, flat-roofed structure, a feed store closed for the night. "Let's get up above, boys," ordered the Ranger as they reached the rear lane.

A boost was enough and when he was up, he gave Buck a hand, then they hoisted the heavy Staples to the tin top. Hurrying to the front edge, they had a first-class seat for the show in the street. Lying flat, they could pick off their foes with little danger of being hit except when they rose up to fire.

Hatfield looked for Ed Tourneau but was unable to pick out Brite's field general. Either the Wasp had retired up the line or had gone around to the back of the houses. Staples, Buck and the tall officer emptied their carbines at the milling horsemen, caught in a crossfire between Evans' defenders and the trio on the roof.

The front door had held and the outlaws did not like the slashing they were receiving. Tourneau had no doubt hoped to catch the cowmen unawares and have an easy time of it with such a large force at his command. Wounded bandits were moving off in retreat, and then eerie screeches, much like Indian war whoops, sounded from the north corner. At this, all ripped rein and spurred away, shooting as they went. A few lifeless marauders were left behind in the dusty haze hanging over the scene.

The Ranger and his two helpers descended and checked up. They sang out to Lucius Evans who cautiously opened the door at Avery's to peek out. Watching for a possible trick and the return of the Wasp, Hatfield crossed and joined the rancher leader. Evans' face was grim.

"Ranger, that was nasty. A slug cut pore Avery. It ain't too bad but I can't impose on him much longer. We've got to make our play pronto." Evans felt guilty at exposing his town friends to such terrible danger. Welder and Kilgore, who had hustled over as the scrap began, appeared from behind the house.

"I'm on my way, suh," nodded Hatfield. "I figger I can beat the Wasp and his crew back to Denison. They'll take their time after the cuttin' up we gave 'em here."

"Fine! It's now or never," cried Lucius Evans.

In the night, Jim Hatfield and Buck rode from Sherman. They picked up speed as they turned their horses toward the mushroom settlement of Denison. Rolled in a wrapper were the posters they had manufactured that afternoon. Hatfield and Evans had made their plans.

A chunk of moon and stars powdering the sky lighted the way. A mile from the junction, Hatfield scented freshly risen dust in the cooling air. "There are riders ahead, Buck. It may be the Wasp and his toughs on

the way home. We'll change course a bit."
He did not wish to run upon Tourneau's
heels as the infuriated outlaws left Sherman
after the stinging defeat.

Not far away lay the road to the Red River
but they held to the rolling plains. Slanting
off the direct route they let Goldy and Old
Heart 7 have their heads. The sorrel would
offer warning if strangers were too near, and
by the moonshine they could distinguish
rougher spots and figures they might overtake.

The lurid yellow glow of Denison hung in
the sky and was visible for miles. As Hatfield and his youthful companion approached, the night wind brought them
strains of fiddles, the raucous voices of men
raised in wassail. They had made a fast run
from Sherman. "I figger we've by-passed
most of Tourneau's bunch," observed the
Ranger. "It will give us time to operate,
before they pull in."

Denison had grown even in the hours
since they had first seen it. New tents and
tarpaulins were up, a confusion of quickly
constructed shelters. Some sort of roof had
been finished on Brite's ugly but roomy
structure. As yet there was no glass in the
gaping, darkened windows. The unpainted
pine boards forming the walls were within a

foot of the portable log shack which Leming Brite had been using as a temporary office as he sold off blocks of range belonging to other men. A lamp, turned low, burned in the smaller edifice and the Ranger decided that Brite had not yet transferred his headquarters.

They skirted the howling, lusty settlement, warily watching for enemies. Without doubt Brite would have held a few gunslingers in Denison although the main bunch had accompanied the Wasp in his attempt to surprise Evans, Welder and Kilgore in Sherman. So long as these three survived, Brite's false claims to the land would be very shaky, and the determined ranchers might raise enough resistance to wreck the Professor's operations.

Coming up behind a long, low building, Hatfield unrolled the signs fetched from Sherman and passed half of them to Buck. They had provided themselves with short nails, and a six-shooter butt served as a good hammer. "You start at the north end, Buck, I'll take the south and we'll meet in the center. Keep away from Brite's office, savvy, I'll deal with that. The Professor must have a guard on duty. Hustle now, before the Wasp pulls in."

"I'll give the Rebel yell, Jim, and look out

past the buildin's on this side in case things get too hot. Adios." The slim youth started off and Hatfield set to work.

There were plenty of handy wooden walls and posts to which he could attach the printed warnings. Bold red or black letters stood out on the white sheets. He tacked one to the front of a cabin on rollers, where the track entered Denison's south terminus, keeping one eye peeled for his foes. It took but a few seconds to put up a sign. He flitted across and left a second, making it fast to a saloon.

The Ranger had thought it out carefully, had designed the notes not only to attract the beholder's attention but to convince and stir up the victims of the land fraud. For the most part he had used large capital letters.

"BEWARE! BRITE IS SELLING YOU OTHER MEN'S LAND!" proclaimed one. Another said, "YOU HAVE BEEN CHEATED! THIS RANGE BELONGS TO L. EVANS, NOT BRITE." A third cried, "BRITE IS OUTLAW, A FRAUD! HE HAS STOLEN YOUR MONEY!"

He had nailed up a dozen, and already curious men, who had seen the tall figure posting the sheets, were gathering to read them. While such people seldom interfered in gun

144

battles in behalf of others, they were easily aroused when it came to defending their own rights. Some were calling to friends to come and see the alarming signs.

The Ranger was almost at the center and not far from Brite's centrally located offices. He glimpsed Buck's bony, tall figure as the youth fastened a warning to a saloon front. A couple of bearded investors came around the corner and surprised Hatfield as he finished putting up a "BEWARE!" job.

"Hey, mister! What's all this?" demanded one, as he hastily took in the gist of it.

"What's the idea!" asked the second.

"That's the truth, boys," replied Hatfield earnestly. "Leming Brite is a thief. He's forged deeds to this range. It ain't his to sell."

Others were staring at the signs which Buck Robertson had left in his wake. A disturbed, menacing buzz of voices rose from the settlement as knots of men collected to talk over the startling news. Many had paid high prices in good money to Brite or to those who had bought from Brite.

Across the square, the Professor appeared against the wide lighted entrance to a honkytonk, Brakeman Karnes hulking at his side. Brite wore his black coat and tall hat, his sidewhiskers shadowing his long face. A

145

six-gun hung in an open holster, the belt tight at his waist.

A couple of minutes before, the Ranger had stuck one of his notices to the front of that honkytonk and somebody had run into the place and warned Brite. The Professor took one horrified look, reached out and ripped the sheet off the wall, crumpling it up and hurling it to the dust.

"It's a lie!" he roared.

Hatfield ducked around the dark side of the Brite Development Company's new quarters. The center of Denison was clogging up as the news spread like wildfire.

The Ranger chuckled to himself. "At least he'll have some tall explainin' to do," he thought.

He hurried to the rear of the building. Through a small window of the portable shack housing Brite's temporary offices, he sighted Yampy, his erstwhile outlaw boss. Yampy was standing up. The fat bandit's face was drawn, worried and he was listening to the new sounds from the populace of the mushroom settlement.

In his hairy, fat hand Yampy gripped a large Colt with a smooth walnut stock, his pet persuader. There was a bandage stuck on one side of his round head, where Ranger lead had singed him up at the Red

River line during the duel with Hatfield. His Stetson, flat-topped and decorated with the Wasp's insignia, hung by its strap from his sagging cartridge belt.

Evidently Yampy had been left to guard the records and office for his injury would have slowed him. Piles of papers, weighted with stones, several boxes, a wooden table with inkwells and pens in the stand, seals and materials needed to fill out documents, benches to use as seats, showed in the single room of the shack. On the crowded table top stood a burning oil lamp with a glass reservoir half filled with kerosene. Yampy limped to the front to peek out at the gathering storm.

Hatfield was at the back. "Yampy!" he called sharply.

The stout killer jumped inches off the dirt floor. He glanced fearfully over a hunched shoulder. "Why, you cussed eyeballer!" he gasped.

"Keep it quiet, Yampy," warned the Ranger. "I'm a lot closer than the last time."

Yampy feared him, having seen him in action, but he was tough. As yet, the officer had no pistol in sight. The stout outlaw dropped to a knee as he whirled, his teeth gritted, and whipped his Colt around.

CHAPTER 12
MELEE

Hatfield was framed like a picture in the window. Once Yampy brought his gun into line he could scarcely miss. It was vital for the officer to fire first. His slim hand blurred with speed and the heavy revolver jumped to his grip, cocking by its own weight as it rose, the hammer spur caught by his thumb joint.

There was a flaming roar and the Colt pushed against the tall man's steady palm. Yampy's muzzle was not quite high enough. The black hole belched fire and metal but it drilled into the dirt floor. Yampy's own impetus as Hatfield's bullet struck kept him lunging forward. He fell hard, sprawling, his clawing hands gripping the table, which overturned. The lamp slid off, glass tinkling. The hot oil caught fire and a licking yellow flame slowly rose. Papers from the upset table began to burn.

"That's not a bad idea at all, Yampy," muttered the Ranger, smoking six-shooter ready.

He could see the stout figure, lying as it had fallen. The outlaw's pistol had flown from his fingers. Hatfield drew aside, took the silver star on silver circle, emblem of the Texas Rangers, from its hidden pocket, pinned it to his shirt front. He checked up again. Yampy was still there and the fire was swiftly gaining.

Confused shouting sounded from across the road and calls from the south. Hatfield squeezed through the small window, a tight fit for the big fellow. His first act was to bend down and make certain Yampy was dead. As Hatfield had believed, the fat gunhand had caught it between the eyes.

He began picking up Brite's records, hurling them into the licking flames. But already the heat, reflected by the log walls, was intense and its searing breath singed him. He shielded his face with an arm and kicked boxes of documents into the heart of the blaze.

The explosions, the dancing light inside his headquarters, had attracted and alarmed Leming Brite. Hatfield saw the Professor and Brakeman Karnes coming as he glanced out the wide counter window in front. They were trailed by many citizens anxious to ask Brite questions about the land they had purchased from the company. Brite pointed at the fired shack, howling in excited fury. The Ranger coughed from coiling smoke, which drafted from the openings. The heat was too much for him and he went out the back way. The Professor's papers were hungrily burning.

A shrill Rebel yell penetrated to him. Buck was calling. He swung and trotted along the line of buzzing structures and tents. His youthful comrade was close at hand, near the spot where they had separated when they had first arrived and gone about posting their bills.

"Jim! I spotted the Wasp down the road. He just hit town with half a dozen of his boys."

"You get mounted and fetch Goldy for me," ordered the Ranger. "I'll be just below Brite's. Hustle."

Buck ran to do his bidding. The tall man hurried south, past the burning shack. A large crowd had already collected, and energetic, quick-thinking men were trying to form bucket brigades to the creek to save the settlement from destruction. Shouts and cursing epithets were raised.

Hatfield appeared on the main stem, coming from between two staked tents. Professor Brite and Brakeman Karnes were caught in the crush in front of the land company's blazing quarters. But Ed Tourneau, the Wasp, mounted on the powerful, long-legged gelding he had used during his raid at Sherman earlier in the evening, was but a few paces from the Ranger's position.

Tourneau was cursing and using his quirt as he sought to work through the thickening crowd, keeping to the edge of the street. Not far behind were several of his outlaw aides. Brite was shouting and signaling frantically to his field general, and the Wasp knew his evil master stood in need of his help.

Suddenly the Wasp spied the tall figure, booted feet spread, close upon him.

"Tourneau!" said Hatfield calmly.

"Texas Ranger!"

The Wasp recognized the star and a shudder of dread shook him. His yellowed, bitter face twisted and he ripped at his rein, rearing his big horse and sliding from his sweated saddle.

A jerk on the rein pulled the excited animal between Tourneau and the officer. Startled inhabitants swung about, saw the big Ranger with the emblem pinned to his shirt, the rugged face, bunched by the taut chinstrap, the icy glint of the gray-green eyes fixed on the Wasp.

For the moment, Tourneau's followers were out of the picture, churning humanity between them and their chief. In that flash of time, a few paces separating the two, it was man to man between the Wasp and the Ranger. Tourneau was snarling, spitting profanity, but he was swift and his hand moved with the dart of a snake's head. The plunging gelding danced sideways, exposing the outlaw.

It was draw to draw. The Rangers gave the worst of killers a chance to surrender, before they would shoot, and Hatfield was no exception. He was calm inside, muscles untensed. A hasty slug from one of the Wasp's friends shrieked over his head but he did not flinch.

Always it was that last fatal breath which counted in such a deadly duel. It was not the man throwing the first slug, but the fighter who maintained a cool brain and dared expend a perilous instant taking careful aim who walked away from these encounters. The Wasp knew this as well as the Ranger did, so for a brief but startling interval of time the two confronted one another, guns out and cocked.

Across the road a dancehall woman on a veranda uttered a shrill scream. Brite and

Brakeman George Karnes were howling, trying to work through the seething gathering. Another bullet from Tourneau's men holed the canvas walls of a tent a few inches from Hatfield.

Then the two opposing Colts flamed apparently at the same click. Something irresistible flicked the cloth bulge of the Ranger's shirt where the tail had worked out during his strenuous exertions in Denison. The Wasp straightened, his bitter mouth snapping wide open as he sought breath that was not for him.

He fired again but the muzzle of his gun was dropping, the murderous metal dully plugging into the earth between Hatfield's spread feet. A bluish hole appeared beside Tourneau's nose. He was mortally hit and his knees gave way. The Ranger's finisher drilled the outlaw chief's body and the Wasp shuddered. He collapsed, landing hard, dead as he folded.

They had seen the Ranger's triumph, the appalling, icy courage of the great officer. Head and shoulders over ordinary men, Jim Hatfield had made the impression he desired in Denison. Admiration for his skill and bravery, respect for the mighty Ranger, welled in the hearts of decent beholders.

Screams of hatred issued from the bearded

throats of the Wasp's gunhands as their leader was worsted in the exchange. "Kill that man! Stop him," shouted Leming Brite, hopping up and down and pointing with his pistol at the officer.

Hatfield was sliding back and several bullets missed him as he moved. In his wide belt was the roll of remaining handbills, warning the public against the operations of Professor Leming Brite and his company. He had thrust them out of the way when he had gone after Yampy at Brite's land headquarters. As he stepped off, he yanked out the posters and flung them over the heads of churning men in the street. The sheets separated, floating down, and eager hands of citizens snatched them.

"Read the truth, boys," he called, his stentorian tones rising over the din. "Brite has robbed you."

"Ranger! Ranger!" That cry was taken up by enthusiastic men. They saw him dart around the back of the tents as a knot of the Wasp's gunhands surged up. A couple of bandits jumped down and bent over the remains of Ed Tourneau.

Texans knew the Rangers, trusted them and counted on them in time of real trouble. There were not many of the state officers, but those operating were famed for honesty, ability and courage. They could not be bribed, and each one was an exceptional person. There was no room in the corps for mediocre men.

Some of the outlaws, entering Denison from the south, and seeing the crush in the center, had started around the buildings and were coming at a fast clip. Guns began flashing.

"Jim! Here we are!" Buck Robertson hailed him. The daring youth had brought Goldy within a few rods of the gunfight. He sat Old Heart 7, the golden sorrel's rein looped over the horn.

Hatfield raised his pistol and sent lead at the dark riders rushing him. Buck began shooting and the rattled bandits swerved, yelling and hunting cover. The glow from Brite's burning offices increased, the light dancing crimson in Denison. In the center the howls and growls of angry citizens joined, and the sound was like that of an infuriated, stirred beehive.

But Leming Brite still had plenty of power, the force to save himself. The brute strength of the Wasp's large band belonged to him. Brakeman George Karnes could command gunsters, and the oversized body-guard jumped into the breach, taking over in Tourneau's place. He bellowed orders to the outlaws and they responded. Mustangs charged the crowds, forcing a path through and before long Brite had a strong circle of bristling, masked killers protecting him.

The Ranger had been pushed away. In the plaza, a leaderless melee surged, unsure of what to do. Everybody had run out to see what was going on. The story of Brite's perfidy had quickly circulated, yet angry as many were, they could not act with the killer guns on them.

Some had formed a bucket line to the creek, fighting the fare which threatened the whole jerry-built settlement. The raw pine wall next the portable shack serving as Brite's office was smoking, flames licking to the roof.

CHAPTER 13
THE NOOSE

Jim Hatfield pelted north behind the building line at Denison. Buck rode just ahead on his chunky, fast gray mustang. The mushroom town was blowing its top with the sudden, terrifying whoosh of an erupting volcano.

"I hope it works the way we figgered," muttered the Texas Ranger. He had timed it as closely as possible under the circumstances. With Brite's gathering strength, Evans and his friends so outnumbered, it had been necessary to arouse the Professor's victims in Denison in order to win enough fighters to smash the Skeleton Riders.

A few hundred yards beyond the outermost buildings, the tall officer began to whistle shrill blasts. From the town's center came a confused babble, and several pistol shots crackled.

Leming Brite had already cleaned up a

small fortune selling lots and parcels of land. No doubt the Professor carried the money on his person as was the habit of such thieves. Brite had expected to take in much more before decamping. If he read the writing on the wall, having seen the Ranger kill Ed Tourneau, and with the populace aroused by Hatfield's broadsides, the Professor would run for it. The Ranger had no intention of permitting his arch-enemy and the bulk of the marauders to escape.

Answering whistles sent him galloping toward a dark brush clump not far away. "Are you there, Mister Evans?" he sang out.

Lucius Evans trotted his mustang from behind the screen, and with him were his fighters, George Welder and Dunc Kilgore, Lake Staples, other cowboys and a dozen friends they had picked up in Sherman.

"We're ready, Ranger," declared Evans, eyes sheening in the faint light.

The stout Welder, the dour Kilgore, flanked the rancher chief. They were prepared to have it out with their enemies, led by Leming Brite and Brakeman Karnes. They had real faith in the Texas Ranger who had come to save them from death and destruction.

"Let's hustle, then," ordered Hatfield, the

star glinting on his shirt front. "String out, fifteen paces between riders. Don't let any of the cusses through but watch out for the folks in town. We don't want to down innocent men and they're on our side."

"Spread out, boys," said Evans, relaying the commands.

Lake Staples moved to a far wing, waddies hurrying into position as the sturdy avengers formed a long line. Welder took the left, Kilgore the right, Evans remaining at the center behind the Ranger on his swift war horse.

Hatfield raised a long arm and threw it forward in the signal to advance. He headed straight down the central way into Denison, followed by his allies. Colts and carbines were held ready for action, the men's faces were grim and set with determination to brace the enemy in this final showdown.

To the officer's right and left, his riders rounded buildings as they held the wide line in formation. The Ranger could see down the long run between unevenly spaced structures and tents to the square. A milling, infuriated crowd filled it. Lanterns strung on poles and the crimson glow of the burning log cabin and new office lighted the scene.

"Here comes the Professor!" sang out Buck.

Leming Brite was on a black horse. He was surrounded by outlaws, many of them with masks adjusted, the flat-crowned Stetsons on. Behind his master was Brakeman George Karnes, turned in his high-pronged saddle, cocked Colt raised as he cursed and threatened the citizens slowly following the retreating band. The Professor had made his choice. He was pulling out while he had the chance; taking what he had won.

Howls of rage issued from bilked victims of Brite's perfidy, but the menacing guns of the bandits cowed them and prevented them from wreaking revenge and capturing Brite. The fact that the Professor was on the run told them that the Ranger's notices were correct. Brite had cheated them.

"Stop him! Arrest Brite," someone screamed frantically.

A knot of men surged forward. Karnes let go with his pistol and a ringleader caught lead, staggered and fell into the arms of his friends. The shooting stopped the advance of the citizens.

The Texas Ranger, his silver star on silver circle pinned to his shirt front, raced in. The cowmen were coming from the darkness and were close upon the marauders before the outlaws, distracted by the dangerous mood of the Denison populace, realized they were at hand. The right and left wings of Hatfield's line, skirting obstructions such as shacks and tents, were hurrying to loop the raiders, noose them as a lasso tightens around its target.

Leming Brite sighted Hatfield and gave a hoarse shout. He pointed a heavy revolver and pulled trigger. The bullet sang over the tall officer's lowered head. The Ranger's Colt snarled a reply and Brite's hat flew from his head. Instead of the full, greased black hair of which the Professor had seemed so vain, Brite's skull shone entirely bald, the taut skin stretched over protruding bumps. Hatfield was startled, then with grim amusement realized the Professor had been wearing a wig which had dislodged along with his hat.

Suddenly aware of the new danger before them, Brite's gunhands faced front, hastily shifting guns. Lucius Evans, Welder and others gave shrill Rebel yells, challenging their opponents.

"Throw down, outlaws," roared the Ranger.

The answer was a blast of metal. Flaming pistol muzzles confronted the charging ranchers who threw back better than they received. Killers in the bunched band holding the middle of the road yelped and swore, recoiling.

"It's the Ranger! Come on, let's give him a hand," shouted a bold Denisonite.

Braver spirits in town rushed forward again. Hatfield's appearance, the mounted fighters behind him, provided the needed spark to ignite the fighting courage of Brite's victims. More and more townsmen started to run after the thieves, gripping clubs and guns. The closing arc ends, cutting between buildings, had almost joined the crush of citizens when Leming Brite ripped rein and smashed off to the right.

Brakeman George Karnes was close to his chief. The two dug spurs. Powerful mustangs surged ahead, and the riders lashed out with gun barrels to make a path for themselves. Several masked outlaws took advantage of the break, spurting in the Professor's wake. Brite and Karnes disappeared from Hatfield's field of vision as they made it safely between two long wooden structures on the east side of Main Street.

Above all, Hatfield wanted Brite. He swung the golden sorrel that way, hoping to overtake the Professor before Brite reached the clear. But the inhabitants of Denison had surged all through the lanes and he was hemmed in, caught in the melee. He could see bearded, excited faces all about him.

The avenging citizens had come up with the blocked killers who had checked their advance as Hatfield and his friends stopped them. Rattled and leaderless, swearing outlaws slashed at the heads and arms of men eagerly pulling them from their saddles. Guns were fired point-blank as the crush grew denser, making it impossible for horses to maneuver.

Excited, plunging mustangs threw several riders busy trying to defend themselves. The skeleton masks were snatched off, weapons confiscated. Lucius Evans, George Welder and Kilgore, with their waddies and townesmen aides from Sherman, were doing their part, fighting the nearest gunslingers to a standstill, holding the half-circle drawn around Denison.

More and more hands clutched the masked marauders. Shouts and blows, explosions, made a horrid din over the mushroom town. But the firing was diminishing. The battle degenerated into a free-for-all as the butts of Brite's great swindle punished the Professor's strongarm assistants, slapped them down, disarmed them and tied them up.

Hatfield edged toward the outer fringe but it was slow going. Buck Robertson, still on Old Heart 7, had downed a couple of bandits but was now pinned by the boiling townsmen. Few of Brite's powerful band remained in sight, and swiftly these were subdued, fright in their burning eyes. They feared lynching at the hands of the angry crowds.

"Hurrah for the Texas Rangers!" shouted a jubilant citizen, who had climbed to a nearby roof top. He waved his Stetson, jumping up and down in excitement.

Men around Hatfield grinned in friendly fashion at the officer who had commanded the forces against the outlaws. With the defeat of the toughs, ropes were brandished over the captured killers, and the Ranger knew that he must check the mob's dangerous mood.

CHAPTER 14
PURSUIT

Gunfire had ceased for all the outlaw targets were down. A few lucky ones had managed to escape with Leming Brite and Brakeman Karnes at the start of the battle. Hatfield felt a sense of urgency, that he must be after Brite, seek to bring back the chief who had brought all this misery on the Red River range.

He stood high in his stirrups, a hand overhead, calling for attention. Those nearest him heard and heeded his authority, ordering others to be quiet. Soon the gathering had stilled, facing him from all directions, watching the rugged face of the ace fighting man.

"You done a fine job helpin' beat those rascals, boys," said the Ranger. "The law will take charge of 'em. Use yore ropes to tie up the cusses. I'll hold to account any man who takes part in lynchin'. Turn the prisoners over to Mister Evans and he'll see they're delivered to the lockup. Brite has run for it. I must go after him and try to fetch him back. Then we'll see what can be done about squarin' accounts for those he cheated.

"All who bought land from Brite's company, hold on to your deeds and I'll straighten things out later. As you have been informed, two railroads will make a junction here at Denison, and maintenance shops are to be built in town so your new settlement will grow fast and amount to somethin'. One line will bridge the Red River, and a span for wagon and horseback traffic will be thrown across the stream, just north of this point.

"All that is true, but Leming Brite was not the owner of the range he sold. He forged the deeds he showed, having forcibly seized lands belongin' to these ranchers. At Brite's command, Ed Tourneau, the Wasp, killed Abel Pyne who held sections needed for the bridge and railroad approaches to the Red River. Hustle, now, reinforce that bucket brigade and check the fire or the whole town will go up in smoke. Mister Evans will be my deputy while I'm gone."

They were ready to obey the Ranger and cheers welled in their throats. Townsmen began shoving their captives to a gathering point, sullen-eyed killers disarmed and help-less with tied hands and guns held on them.

Buck Robertson rode to join Hatfield as he swung out of Denison. "Have you seen Lake Staples?" asked the Ranger.

"Not since the start of it," replied Buck. "He was over on the east."

"Brite broke clear that way. I hope nothin' happened to Lake."

He cut over, followed by his youthful comrade, and rode down the line. A crumpled figure lay in the shadows and they feared it might be Staples but dismounting and checking, Hatfield found it was a dead outlaw, skeleton mask awry on his evil face. He recognized one of the bandits he had met at the hideout north of the Red.

Remounting, he started to shove north-ward. The river lay four miles away, with not much rough country between. Bathed in faint silver moonlight, the rolling plains swept in almost imperceptible drops toward the Red.

"What makes you figger Brite came this direction, Jim?" asked Buck curiously.

"I believe he'll make for the Territory," answered Hatfield. "No law over there, for one thing, and there's plenty of spots where he can hole up to catch his breath. Of course, he may have turned another way but I'll have to chance it."

To follow sign in the night was difficult, and very slow. The tracker must dismount every few yards and check up. By that time, Brite would have made too many miles. The two moved along at a fast clip. As they neared the spot where the ferry crossed the river, Hatfield sniffed at the fresh dust hanging in the air. "Somebody came along here not so long back," he remarked.

The golden sorrel rippled his hide, and they slowed, watching. Against the moonlit sky toward the Red a rider appeared, and they sat their saddles, motionless, guns ready for action. Soon the horseman spied them and pulled up.

"Who's that?" demanded the Ranger.

"Hatfield!" Lake Staples hurried up to them. "I trailed Brite and Brakeman Karnes, with four of the Wasp's crew, to the river. They swam it a quarter of an hour ago. I couldn't stop the cusses."

Hatfield was glad to receive this news of Brite's progress. He had guessed the Professor's escape route correctly.

"You goin' over, Jim?" inquired Buck.

"I'm goin' over," nodded the Ranger.

He could not permit Leming Brite to go free. Texas law did not hold in the Territory but the law of self-defense did, no matter where it might be invoked.

They pushed on, Staples joining them, and soon came to the edge of the Red, flowing slowly in the moonlight. The saloon and little store were dark, the low, flat ferry boat warped to the Texas shore for the night. The one-eyed Mexican and the operators of the ferry slept.

Hatfield rode the golden sorrel into the shallows, Staples and Buck following. They swam the channel and the dripping mustangs dug in their hoofs on the north bank, hitting the winding road.

"We'll try the Wasp's hideout first," announced Hatfield.

He rode ahead, alert for drygulchers on the trail. Buck came next, with Lake Staples bringing up the rear. In the distance, a wolf howled mournfully at the moon.

Close to the Wasp's headquarters in the bush, the Ranger got down and spoke to his two loyal comrades, voice low. "Buck, hold the horses. Lake, can you limp along and cover me? I'm goin' in after the Professor."

"I can make it, Ranger," nodded Staples.

The main band smashed, the Wasp, Yampy and their old leaders killed in the fight at Denison, only a handful of the once mighty outlaw aggregation remained at the hideout.

Some who had managed to flee from the Ranger and the crowd at the new settlement had not yet stopped, were making for tall timber far away, having had enough.

Armed with his Colts, the tall officer flitted around through the bush, familiar with the surroundings. Lanterns flickered in the camp and as he crouched close to the clearing to look things over, Hatfield spied lathered, heaving horses, one of them Brite's long-legged black, standing with dropped head. They had been quirted and spurred to a frazzle as the Professor made his desperate lunge to escape.

There was a lamp burning in the larger hut which had belonged to the Wasp, and which Brite had shared with the outlaw chief. The Ranger circled to the rear but froze in his tracks as he heard stealthy footsteps. Three dark figures rounded the headquarters and stole down the back trail toward the horse corrals. They passed within a few feet of the hidden officer.

One said, "Keep it quiet! We better get out of here, you can't tell what's goin' to happen, boys."

They disappeared toward the pens. The Ranger decided they had heard the story of the defeat at Denison and were decamping to save their hides. Law or not, a posse might cross and come after them. They were older men who had been left to guard the camp.

The Ranger let them go, having Brite on his mind. He inched to the little window at the back and peeked inside. Brakeman Karnes, hulking figure girded with two cartridge belts, was packing a bag. Brite, his bald pate sheening, had just taken a pinch of snuff and sneezed several times. The Professor seemed satisfied with himself. He poured a stiff drink into a tin mug and downed it at a gulp.

"It isn't so bad, George," he remarked. "We have enough to live like kings for a while. We'll go back to New Orleans and play the wheels."

"You aim to start tonight?" asked the Brakeman.

"Certainly. That Texas Ranger doesn't look like he'd stop at the Red River line." Brite patted his bulging shirt sides. "I flatter myself I outwitted him. Hurry, now. Pick out two good horses from the pens and we'll start for Kansas. At railhead we can entrain for St. Louis and catch the cars there for the South."

"Want to take along any of these hombres in camp?"

"No. They're no use to me now. We'll leave 'em behind."

Brite drank again, smacking his lips. His teeth clicked and he pulled at his sidewhiskers, eyes bright as polished shoe-buttons.

The Ranger glided around to the open door and stepped inside.

The Professor saw him first and his long face twisted in astonishment. "Ranger!"

Hatfield stood there, slim hands hanging easily at his hips. As yet he had not drawn a Colt. "Howdy, Professor!" he drawled.

"You can't arrest me here! You have no jurisdiction," babbled Brite.

"You savvy the law even if you do break it whenever you've a mind to, Bright Eyes," replied the Ranger. "I'll tote you across the Red and arrest you in Texas if that suits you better."

The Brakeman thought he saw his chance. Brite stood between the door and Karnes, who lunged with a hoarse battle cry, pistol ripping from leather holster. The heavy gun was coming up to drill Hatfield at close range.

Feet spread, Hatfield's hand flicked, blurred with its speed. The Brakeman's charge was checked; he shuddered as the cabin filled with the reverberating explosion, and dropped hard, face to the dirt floor.

Leming Brite knew what the silver star on silver circle meant, that the tall officer who had relentlessly opposed and pursued him, would forcibly take him back to justice. He had a breath in which to act and seized it as Hatfield dueled with Karnes. With remarkable celerity, the Professor pulled a snubnosed pistol from the holster under his bony arm.

The Ranger felt the wind of passing metal. He had to shoot quickly, for Brite, teeth clicking, his eyes blazing, shrieked at him as he thrust the muzzle of the gun straight at Hatfield's face, at point-blank range.

Hatfield's Colt blared, once, and again. The revolver was steady, his aim cool and unflurried in spite of the death only a wink away. Brite caught the slugs in the body. He was turned by the impact, and his right arm fell, an amazed expression coming over the long face. His knees buckled and he folded up before his master, the Texas Ranger.

Denison had quieted down some as Jim Hatfield, Lake Staples and Buck Robertson rode into the center. Behind the Ranger was a led horse carrying the remains of Professor Leming Brite.

Staples and Buck had rushed into the outlaw hideout as they heard the shooting. The handful of bandits had not put up much of a scrap, but had run for the dark bush.

The fire had been controlled, kept from spreading by the bucket brigades, although Brite's log cabin and the new headquarters had burned to the ground. All the false records had gone up in flames, and that was just as well, thought Hatfield.

Lucius Evans hailed him gladly, and soon the ranchers and their cowboys surrounded the returning trio, staring at the dead Professor. Citizens of Denison, emerging from saloons where they had been drinking after the battle, hurried to see the Ranger and what was left of Brite.

Hatfield took a chair on a porch overlooking the center. He had bulky money-bags in hand, which he had removed from around Brite's waist, and these contained the Professor's loot from his venture in Denison.

"Spread the word, boys," ordered the tall officer. "We'll set things as straight as we can, here and now."

Buck found a barrel for him and he used it as a table. Lines were formed, and those who had bought land from Leming Brite waited their turn as the Texas Ranger dispensed what he had recovered. He paid according to the deeds and receipts signed by Brite, satisfying as many claims as possible.

It was very late when he had finished his task. "All right, gents. You have your money back, far as I can make it. If you want to buy land here, talk to the real owners, these ranchers." He nodded and rose, stretching himself. A drink was in order, and his job on the Red River range had come to a close.

Reporting at Captain Bill McDowell's headquarters in Austin, Jim Hatfield saluted his chief and dropped into a chair by the desk. Buck and Anita Robertson were safe at home in the cottage on the outskirts of the capital.

"So Miss Anita fetched my message concernin' the bridges over the Red River and the railroads?"

"Yes, suh. I was glad to have it, Cap'n, for it corroborated what I'd learned from studyin' Brite's papers. Through skulduggery and bribery in New Orleans, that Professor snake had obtained secret, advance information as to just where the junction of the rails would be, not far from Lucius Evans' home. Shops were to be built and the rights-of-way would cross the Slash K and 1–2, the spans over the Red based on land belongin' to a citizen of Sherman, Abel Pyne.

"Brite wrote his man, the Wasp, to kill the range owners pronto before the news leaked out to the public and the boom began. Tourneau managed to kill Pyne, droppin' Brite's note which Marshal Suyderman sent on to us. Then they went after the ranchers and drove 'em from their houses."

McDowell listened to the terse sentences as the Ranger told of the fighting on the Red River. His old eyes glistened with excitement for he could read between the lines, knowing what desperate battles had taken place and wishing he had been there to take part in them. He was satisfied to hear that Brite's false records had burned to ashes, that the Ranger had made restitution as far as was humanly possible, that Lake Staples, the cowboy who had done so well for his employer, had married his boss' daughter in Sherman, with Anita and Hatfield among the audience.

But Texas called. Over its mighty expanse, a few Rangers must uphold the law. While Hatfield had been out on duty, new complaints had come in and Captain McDowell rattled the stack on his desk.

"I'm ready, suh. My wound's healin' fine, thanks to Miss Anita's care. Goldy is rested and we can ride."

Soon the old commandant stood in his doorway, waving adios to his star operative who carried justice to the Lone Star State.

We hope you have enjoyed this Large Print book. Other Thorndike, Wheeler, Kennebec, and Chivers Press Large Print books are available at your library or directly from the publishers.

For information about current and upcoming titles, please call or write, without obligation, to:

Publisher
Thorndike Press
295 Kennedy Memorial Drive
Waterville, ME 04901
Tel. (800) 223-1244

or visit our Web site at:

http://gale.cengage.com/thorndike

OR

Chivers Large Print
published by BBC Audiobooks Ltd
St James House, The Square
Lower Bristol Road
Bath BA2 3SB
England
Tel. +44(0) 800 136919
email: bbcaudiobooks@bbc.co.uk
www.bbcaudiobooks.co.uk

All our Large Print titles are designed for easy reading, and all our books are made to last.